THE WOMAN IN
White Marble

ALSO BY DALE ROMINGER

Nonfiction
Notes from 39,000 Feet
Dis-Ease: Living with Prostate Cancer

Fiction
Alien Love or Thank You Alpha Centauri

Visit Dale Rominger's Website
The Back Road Café
(www.thebackroadcafe.com)

THE WOMAN IN
White Marble

Dale Rominger

DALE ROMINGER

iUniverse

The Woman in White Marble

iUniverse books may be ordered through booksellers or by contacting:

iUniverse
1663 Liberty Drive
Bloomington, IN 47403
www.iuniverse.com
1-800-Authors (1-800-288-4677)

ISBN: 978-1-4917-4281-5 (sc)
ISBN: 978-1-4917-4282-2 (hc)
ISBN: 978-1-4917-4280-8 (e)

Library of Congress Control Number: 2014914251

Printed in the United States of America.

iUniverse rev. date: 08/28/2014

To Peter, a gentleman and a friend, who
wrote in his last "jottings":

Patience, Understanding, Forgiveness, Friendliness
Live Simply, Love Generously, Care Deeply, Speak Kindly

1

The name is Drake. Drake Ramsey. People call me Drake. This is a true story. I'm not handing you that old "based on a true story" crap. Nor is this a Coen brothers' *Fargo*esque misdirection. Trust me. I'm telling it straight up. This *is* the story—and believe you me, it's a story worth telling. Murder, a marble statue with a past, and one hell of a sexy ghost.

I'm a reporter and now a novelist. I prefer to call myself a reporter rather than a journalist, reasons for which you will understand as you get to know me. And in the spirit of "straight up," I guess I'm not really a novelist if the definition of a novelist is a person who has written a novel. I have begun writing a novel, though, so that should count for something.

I've been working on an idea for a novel for some years. When I say "working on an idea for years," I mean I've been *thinking* about the idea. I didn't actually start writing until I arrived in this godforsaken

I

place at the edge of the world. My idea is a kind of Proust-in-outer-space story. It's perfectly clear that if you want to write a novel critiquing the socioeconomic political state of America, science fiction is the only legitimate way to go. Obviously I had to read *In Search of Lost Time*. I had heard that if you could actually finish the damn thing (it's eight volumes!) it would be a profound experience. Oh wait. It's six volumes. Just felt like eight. It was a challenge, I have to say. In one of the volumes, can't remember which, Proust went on about a party for a couple hundred pages. One party!

After eight months of reading, I had reached the denouement in the last volume on a flight from San Francisco to Miami. An old guy sitting next to me kept turning his cell phone on and off, which in those days was a big no-no. I finally asked him what he was doing, explaining it wasn't safe, and he said, "I like watching the time zones change." Very Proustian, but not really the way I had imagined finishing Proust. Life, hey.

I'm going to have to come up with some kind of futuristic, outer-space madeleine sponge cake, which is proving to be a real challenge. I have, however, worked out the name of my main protagonist: Chad Steel. Get it? Chad Steel. Charles Swann. C. S.

This place. I guess it wasn't the brightest thing to have made the arrangements on the Internet, though I do pride myself on my investigative skills. This is a lost place at the end of time. Or a lost-in-time place at the end of the world. I guess both, really. The first few days were such a downer I decided I had "to embrace the reality"—something I imagine Chad Steel will be very good at.

I heard some people talking in the post office about how great the ice cream is in Allonby, a coastal town not far down the road from here. Apparently Allonby ice cream is uniquely good, amazingly good, so I jumped in my car, a piece of red junk with a leaky floor and no brakes to speak of, also acquired on the Internet.

When I got to Allonby, I discovered a middle-aged man with a soft ice cream machine! It was raining, and people were standing around eating soft fucking machine ice cream as if they were in paradise. Can you imagine?

I was so disappointed I was about to get in my car and return to Silloth when I realized that would definitely not be "embracing the reality." You see, I remembered an old movie, something about an American who worked for an oil company, I think, and was sent to some Scottish island. After the cultural shock passed, he embraced the reality of his situation. Very romantic. I thought that could be the answer for me. Romanticize this dreary, windswept place. I imagined it: me at the end of the world, "embracing the reality." I crossed the street and walked onto the beach and looked out to sea. It seems to me the guy in the movie did that. I stood there, the rain pouring down, the wind trying to blow me over and coming damn close to succeeding. The cold penetrating to my bones. Romantic? Talk about nonsense.

By the time I returned to Silloth and parked in front of the house I was renting, the rain had stopped, and parents were collecting their kids from school. My house was one among six in a row looking over the Solway Firth. Mine was the one next to the end house, which in turn was next to a small road leading to the local school for little kids. As I got out of my car, a mother was standing on the sidewalk, yelling at her little boy. "You filthy boy! What is wrong with you?" she shouted for all the world to hear.

The little guy was looking up at his mother, holding his crotch, crying and shouting, "Cut it off, Mummy! Cut it off!"

I kid you not.

"You're a filthy boy, wetting your trousers like that. You should be ashamed of yourself. How do you think I feel? I'm humiliated."

"Cut it off, Mummy! Cut it off!"

Welcome to Silloth.

My house was narrow, too narrow. And tall, too tall. Three stories of narrow and tall. The rooms on the first and second floors were arranged three in a row, front to back. It came furnished but in a special Silloth kind of way. On the first floor the front room had a couch so filthy that I couldn't bring myself even to touch it, let alone sit on it. Next to the couch was a chair with the stuffing coming out of the right arm. I can't begin to describe the rug, but you would not have wanted to go barefoot. There was a large bay window and a fireplace that was blocked up. The walls were not so much off-white as dirty white. The middle room in the row was the dining room, and the third, at the back of the house, the kitchen. Attached to the ceiling of the kitchen was a gizmo with a pulley system that I learned was for drying your clothes. Pin your clothes to the gizmo and pulley it up to the ceiling. Since I was only planning to be in town for six months, I had to use the damn thing. What could I do? I gotta tell you, it was hard getting into my jeans after they had been hanging from the ceiling. Stiff as a board. As for my underwear, I don't even want to talk about it.

I made the second floor my home. The staircase was steep and long. The damn thing creaked. Upstairs, I used the front room as a living and dining area. The room had a small couch and lounge chair, TV, bookcase, dining table, and two dining chairs. There was a bay window, smaller than the one downstairs, that looked out over a couple of tennis courts and the Solway Firth. On a clear day I could see Scotland across the water, which meant I very rarely ever saw Scotland.

I put the large chair near the window and the couch along the wall facing the TV. I had a few books in the bookcase but no knickknacks of any kind. I didn't plan on being there that long. Above the bookcase was a painting of the Solway. The painting was

ISLAND BOOKS

3014 78TH AVE SE
MERCER ISLAND WA 98040
206-232-6920
www.islandbooks.com

749688 Reg 1 3:29 pm 05/20/18

S FIRE & FURY INSID	1 @	30.00	30.00
S GIRL IN THE SILVE	1 @	13.99	13.99
S WOMAN IN WHITE MA	1 @	13.95	13.95
SUBTOTAL			57.94
SALES TAX - 10%			5.79
TOTAL			63.73
CREDIT CARD PAYMENT			63.73

FREE GIFT WRAP & FREE U.S. SHIPPING

Thanks to all the voters who made us
the #1 BOOKSTORE in this year's
KING5 BEST OF WESTERN WASHINGTON poll!

grotesque. It was not signed. I assumed the painter was protecting his reputation. In between the TV and bookshelf was a fireplace converted to a gas fire. The TV, bookcase, and fireplace were all on the wall I shared with my neighbors. Sometimes when it was quiet, I could hear one of them winding what I learned was a grandfather clock. The sound was somehow comforting.

The next room in the row I used as my study, and the back room my bedroom. The bed was so bad, and I mean really bad, I took it downstairs and dumped it in the front room. I went to Carlisle, to a place that employed disabled people. I got a good but inexpensive bed, and they got work. I was supposed to sand and finish the head- and footboards, but I couldn't be bothered and just put the thing together. Living on the middle floor worked well, though admittedly the kitchen was downstairs. I never went up to the top floor.

After dinner on my fifth day in Silloth, the sun came out, which I assumed would have been headline news if Silloth had a newspaper. I put on my coat, took a chair from the kitchen, and sat out on the front stoop. Across the street, Dr. Pritchard was playing tennis. Dr. Pritchard is the head doc in the only doctors' office in town, called "the surgery" by the natives. I met the doc when registering for medical care. He played tennis most every day. I knew this because, while I had only been in town for five days, from my upstairs front window I had seen Dr. Pritchard play tennis on four of them. The thing about Dr. Pritchard was that when he served, he foot faulted every time! Foot fault: What am I saying? By the time he came down, he was a quarter of the way into the court. He body faulted! And no one ever called him on it, ever. Drove me crazy! I was supposed to be writing the Proustian sci-fi novel of the decade, and all I could do was sit there watching this idiot body fault. I felt like going downstairs, out the front door, over to the courts, and yelling, "Fucking foot fault, you dick!"

You see how distracting Dr. Pritchard could be, so much so that I found it difficult to get into my writing. Anyway, as I sat there on the front stoop watching Pritchard body fault, a young guy, must have been about eighteen years old, came walking up the street and stopped in front of my house. He looked at me and said, "Hi, I'm Leon." This came as a surprise to me. Leon was the first person who spoke to me who didn't have to.

"I saw you in the Spar the other day, then in old man Cartwright's shop buying bowls. What the hell are you doing here?" Leon wasn't being aggressive, just curious.

"I'm writing a novel and wanted to be somewhere quiet, where not too much happens, so I wouldn't be distracted and could concentrate on my writing," I said.

"Well, you fucking got that right, man. No fucking thing ever happens here."

Leon laughed and looked out across the Solway and said, "We do have beautiful sunsets … but who gives a fuck?" He then turned back to me and said, "I'm getting the fuck out of here next week. I'm quitting my job and going to Italy."

"What are you going to do in Italy?" I asked.

"Fuck if I know. But I won't be doing it here!" Leon seemed pretty damn determined.

"Where do you work?" I asked for no particular reason.

"The Skinburness Hotel. I clear tables and wash dishes. It's a nice place."

The words "nice place" caught my attention. To be honest I doubted Leon could be telling the truth. So far I hadn't seen anything nice in this edge-of-nowhere town. But I asked anyway, "Where's the Skinburness Hotel?"

"In Skinburness, just a mile up the road," he said pointing to my right.

With that, Leon said his good-byes, and I never saw him again. As he walked away I had this terrible premonition that years from now I'd be sitting on this same stoop, looking at the who-gives-a-fuck sunsets. Suddenly I had a strong urge to run, run anywhere, as long as it was away from Silloth.

2

P erhaps a little bit of my backstory would be helpful, explaining how I got here. Before all this started—Silloth, the Skinburness Hotel, the Woman in White Marble—I was a reporter on the *Fremont Argus News* in Northern California. I cut my teeth on the *Union City Gazette*, then moved up to the *Fremont Argus News*. From my early days as a student in the College of Hayward journalism department, I imagined myself bringing down bankers and presidents. As it turned out, I spent most of my time rewording Reuters wire stories, then slipping in my byline. The hardest-hitting story I did for the *Fremont Argus News* was a probing investigation into Fremont councilmen and women feuding over where they parked their cars. Sex and money it wasn't. Local governments, hey.

I was living with my woman friend, Kaitlyn Lethbridge, in Union City. I say "woman friend" because she would have sued me if I had called her my girlfriend. One day she came home and went straight into the bedroom without saying a word. I was sitting in the kitchen, reading the *Fremont Argus News*, which admittedly didn't take all that long, given 70 percent of the paper was advertising, keeping one eye on the dinner I was preparing on the stove. Just as I was about to finish with the *Fremont Argus News*, Kaitlyn came into the kitchen, dressed to kill. She just stood by the sink, looking at me.

Bright red stilettos. A tight black skirt that emphasized her rather wonderful butt and left it in no doubt the woman had legs all the way to the top. A beige blouse that was so sheer you could see her pure white, sexy lace bra. It was hard not to be impressed, though it did seem a bit over-the-top for dinner around the kitchen table.

"What's up?" I asked.

"Drake, John said he would help me with my brief, but we'd have to do it over dinner. The trial's in two weeks," she said, looking me straight in the eyes. Kaitlyn is a lawyer and John a senior partner in the firm. Kaitlyn's on a fast track to glory.

"And it's important for John's concentration that your bra is on show?"

"Drake, for God's sake."

"And what about dinner? I've prepared stuffed peppers and—"

"What'd you stuff them with? Hamburger meat?" she interrupted. "You cook everything with hamburger meat. My God, I'm sick of hamburger meat!"

She looked down at the floor for a moment and then suddenly lifted her head in a dramatic motion and said, "Drake, we have to talk."

That usually meant she had to talk and I had to listen. I knew I was in some kind of shit because she kept starting sentences with my name. And just for the record, I do not cook everything with hamburger meat. Sure, I like hamburger meat, but I definitely do *not* cook everything with hamburger meat. I'm just saying for the record.

9

"Drake. You don't stimulate me. You don't stimulate me intellectually. You don't stimulate me sexually. Why?"

That was a rhetorical question. She continued without taking a breath. "Because you're boring. Boring. Boring! *Boring!* Drake. We're through. I want you out of here as soon as possible."

It was her house.

Me boring. Me, a reporter on the mean streets of Fremont and Union City, California. I think not.

Be that as it may, she turned and walked from the kitchen, through the dining room, to the living room, and out the front door. Red fuck-me shoes, swaying ass, and delicate bra straps mocking me all the way. I thought about shouting something about "briefs." Get it? A play on the words *brief* and *briefs*, her being a lawyer and all dolled up. However, I rose above the temptation. Besides, I assumed she was going commando.

It took me a couple of days to get my bearings, which I did in the privacy of the guest bedroom. I decided to call my best friends Gerard and Abigail Schleiermacher. As I thought they would, they insisted I stay in their guest bedroom. It was there that I rose to the challenge and thought about my future. Instead of being crushed, I grabbed hold of the tail of life and ran with it. Well, you know what I mean. In no time at all I had a plan.

First, I had a yard sale on Kaitlyn's front lawn to rid myself of possessions I no longer needed. What was needed I temporarily stored in Gerard and Abigail's garage.

Second, I took a leave of absence from my job at the *Fremont Argus News*. My grandmother had died a couple of years back and left me with a nice little sum. It wasn't enough to propel me into the 1 percent. Nothing like that. But it did give me some breathing space.

Third, I decided to devote six months to writing my novel, the

Proustian sci-fi epic. I figured six months would get Chad Steel around the galaxy, madeleine sponge cake or not.

Fourth, to guarantee my complete concentration on the task of writing, I decided to move to England. I thought the change would do me good. New start and all that. And I liked England, despite the fact that Kaitlyn and I had a really big, fucking fight on an ancient wall surrounding ancient York. I did my research, homing in on a place that would promise isolation from the distractions of civilization. I came up with a small town on the Solway Firth called Silloth that seemed to guarantee solitude.

It was a plan.

On the day before my flight to London, I had one last and very painful task. I had to abandon my Toyota Corolla, a most loyal car. The odometer was approaching 175,000 miles. The tires were worn. The dashboard was cracked and peeling from years of hot sun beating through the windshield. The gray paint was pitted and had lost its luster years ago. And there was a bullet hole in the roof on the driver's side. Now that's an interesting tale that led to an in-depth story in the *Fremont Argus News*.

A couple of years ago Gerard and I were standing by the Corolla parked in front of Kaitlyn's house. Kaitlyn kept her car in the driveway and didn't like me blocking her in. I had my hand on the roof of the car when all of a sudden we heard a *whoosh* and a *bam!* Right by my hand was a bullet hole, the bullet now embedded in the roof. Some asshole had shot his gun into the air, not thinking or not caring that the bullet had to come down, which it did into my car. Gerard and I pondered, both individually and collectively, that if the bullet had come down a foot either to the right or left, one of us could have been killed. It makes you think. I mean, we didn't turn to Jesus or anything, but still. The readers of the *Fremont Argus News* got a shocking story about the number of deaths in the

United States caused by bullets falling out of the sky. Okay, I admit there aren't any reliable statistics on this, but it's gotta be a lot. I'm just saying. You know what the other word for journalism is? That's right. *Speculation.*

Anyway, Gerard and I went online and found a place that advertised "Money for Any Car!! Ask for Joe," which sounded like just the ticket. I drove Old Gray to the place in South Berkeley, with Gerard following behind in his Dodge Dart, also an incredibly loyal automobile. When I got to the place, I asked Joe how much he would give me for my car.

"I can't give you any money for that thing," Joe said, looking at Old Gray and shaking his head.

"What do you mean? Your ad says money for *any* car!" I said, not a little distressed and angry.

"I know, but I can't give you money for *that.* I'd lose on the deal." Joe actually laughed at this point.

I was pissed as hell, but I was also flying out the next morning. If the mean streets had taught me anything, it was when it's time to cut your losses and run. I looked at Gerard, at the ground, then at Joe. "Would you take if off my hands for fifty dollars?"

What could I do?

3

It had been three weeks since my conversation with Leon, and true to his word, he split town and headed to Italy, or so said my neighbor Kelly Tilford. I learned fairly quickly that Kelly was the go-to girl in Silloth if you wanted information, though, of course, I've got a nose for that sort of thing too. You know, who in the streets can give you the dirty lowdown. Kelly and Parker Tilford lived next door. They had the end house, which was considerably bigger than mine. Parker was the quiet, reflective, intellectual type. Hell, one night we sat up till three in the morning drinking whiskey, and he compiled a list of books I *had* to read before I die, for my enlightenment. In his spare time he studies for extra degrees through correspondence courses. That's right. He's that smart. Kelly is smart too, but a different kind of smart: the kind of smart you could take to the bank. If you wanted to get something done, Kelly was your girl.

Kelly, bless her, did what she could to integrate me into the community. One day she dropped by and convinced me to go to a rummage sale in one of the local churches. Kelly's a practicing Catholic. I'm not practicing anything. But I decided the distraction would be healthy, and I owed a lot to Kelly. We went to a church called St. Andrew's, which was the local United Reformed church, not Kelly's Catholic church. When I asked what a good Catholic girl was doing in a Protestant church, Kelly explained that *all* the churches had rummage sales, and the members of these churches went to *all* of the sales to be supportive. There were seven churches in Silloth, so that's a lot of rummage sales.

I said, "Let me get this straight. You go to all the churches' rummage sales and buy stuff, and they come to your rummage sale and buy stuff."

"That's right," she said.

"Well, why don't you all give the money you spend in these rummage sales to your own church and stop having the sales?" I asked.

"Because they are also important social events."

"Then why don't you all pool your efforts and give the money to charity?"

"You're a bloody sinner, Drake Ramsey," she said, laughing as she walked away.

The sociological and anthropological implications of this behavior struck me as profound. And not a little like a Woody Allen movie. I thought, *Make a mental note. Possible interesting and exotic special feature for the* Fremont Argus News.

I have to confess, and I'm not proud of this, that the writing hadn't been going very well up to that point. I'd sit in the front chair by the bay window, laptop balanced on my knees. Most days it was raining horizontally, the wind blowing like there was no tomorrow.

The gray sky crushed down on the land and sea alike. My damn windows rattled. But I knew dear old Granny would be pleased I was thinking about working some. "Boy, you've got to make a living before my money runs out," I could hear her whispering in my ear each day.

Looking out my window to the left was a stand of tall trees filled with big black birds that seemed to take pleasure in shitting on my car. The natives said that if the birds shit on your car, it was good luck. Can you believe that? I gotta tell you, in Union City shit is shit. Apparently, once a year the men in this dreary place were allowed to get their guns out and shoot as many birds as they could. Either the birds were very good at reproducing, or the men were damn poor shots, because my car was always covered in shit.

There was an old man I could see wandering up and down the street. I first saw him from my window. Each day he went to Kelly and Parker's door, trying to enter. Kelly explained to me that he used to be the vicar of the Church of England in town, and their house used to be the vicarage back in those days. He never left Silloth and now wandered all over town, mumbling to himself. For some reason not worth exploring, the guy kind of scared me, and don't forget I've been around the block a few times. I watched him in his black coat, shoulders bent, shuffling along in his burdensome shoes, and every time this heavy shadow settled over me like a dark cloak. I saw myself as the old man, trapped in Silloth in some kind of *Twilight Zone* altered reality, wandering up and down this gray, windy hellhole.

One day when I was out for a walk, just as I was passing him on the sidewalk, he stopped, leaned his face in *real close* to mine, and said, "She was so white!"

"Who was so white?" I asked, but wanted to shout, *Hey buddy, personal space! Get your face out of mine. I can fucking smell your rotten breath, you old freak.*

Anyway he just looked at me with his eyes all watery and said, "She was."

What the shit! This town. Let's call it Freaktown-on-the-Solway. Leon had the right idea.

So I was sitting in my chair with my laptop on my knees, wondering if Chad Steel would like madeleine sponge cake, listening to the wind and rain on my windows, getting sucked into some deep, black vortex by that old vicar, when I remembered what Leon had said about the hotel he worked in. Frankly, Leon was a bit of a weird kid, so I realized that what was nice to him could be a dump to me. But I'd been in dumps before, so I figured what the hell. I decided to get off my ass and head up to the Skinburness Hotel.

As it turned out, Skinburness was a tiny hamlet only a mile up the road. Just as you reached the hotel, the road took a sharp right-angle turn. Don't turn and you would drive in the front door of the hotel. I slid my red, bird-crap-covered excuse for an automobile into the lot, shook the water sloshing on the floor off my shoes, and had a look around. Skinburness made Silloth look like a metropolis. There were only a few houses and barns, and it looked like half the village drowned some time ago. But happily, Leon was right. The Skinburness Hotel was real nice.

The bar area was to the right as I entered the front door. It was warm and the windows didn't rattle. On that, my first visit, I did a quick look around, taking everything in, as is my way. The room was well lit but not too bright. This was obviously the area for light meals, but it was no pub. Everything shouted *nice hotel*. I assumed there was an upmarket restaurant somewhere else.

I saw a long, handsome wooden bar staffed by a young woman smiling at me. She said hello and I smiled back. There were a few good bitters on offer and enough spirits behind her to satisfy the Sixth Fleet. To the left of the bar was a small table occupied by a young couple drinking bottled Bud. Bud is *expensive* in these parts. I wanted to tell the couple that back home, Bud was a cheap drunk.

To my right, in the large front window, was a table for four, and there were three smaller tables for two on the far wall. Around the end of the bar were two more tables for four, one in a secluded alcove. The carpet was a warm green and looked damn plush. The whole place felt nice.

I went to a small table near the front window and threw my coat on one of the chairs and my newspaper on the table. I always take a newspaper when I'm eating on my own. It offers good cover as I case a place. I walked up to the bar and got a great smile for my trouble. I only wished she were a little older. Age isn't everything, but it certainly is something. And when you're pushing forty, you don't sweet-talk an eighteen-year-old, even if she isn't jailbait. Still, I appreciated the smile. I knew I'd take it home with me.

I told her I'd have a pint of what the locals drank. She lifted a glass, still smiling, and put her left hand on the wooden pump labeled *Choice*. It turned out to be a damn good beer. She told me they offered table service, and sure enough, another pretty young thing was at my side by the time I unfolded the paper.

As I was reading my paper and drinking my beer, I noticed a tall, silver-haired man in a good suit enter the bar. He spoke to the woman behind the bar as he looked around the room. He briefly made eye contact with me, offering a smile and a nod. I acknowledged his greeting and surreptitiously went back to my paper. A few minutes later he left. Given his demeanor and the barmaid's body language, I judged he was the manager or owner or both. I was, of course, right—it's what I do. However, confirmation would have to wait for another couple of weeks. That night, as I sat there with my pint and my paper, I had no idea what this silver-haired gentleman was going to drag me into.

4

When I'd been in Silloth for just over five weeks, I thought, *Well, why not have madeleine sponge cake in outer space?* The truth was, I was struggling. I'd never actually tasted madeleine sponge cake or even ever smelled the damn stuff. I mean, how often does a streetwise reporter for the *Fremont Argus News* run into madeleine sponge cake? That's right. Fucking never. And, of course, my chances of finding madeleine sponge cake in Silloth were absolute zero. I had to google the damn stuff to find out what it looked like. I have to say, once I found out, I had a hard time imagining Chad Steel eating it.

On top of that, I'd never traveled throughout the galaxy in a spaceship, so you can see I was having trouble relating. I did decide that Chad Steel has a beard, is ruggedly handsome with broad shoulders, and stands about six-two. He exudes confidence without arrogance, unless complete confidence over his enemies can be considered arrogant. To say he is intelligent is a gross understatement that can only be considered insulting. If you are looking for a hero—a real hero, not some cartoon, cardboard cut-out hero—then you need look no further than Chad Steel.

However, I wasn't getting anywhere sitting by the window, and it was time to put on the old feedbag, so I grabbed my authentic black Moleskine and my coat and headed down to the Skinburness. My plan was to sit and think with a pint of beer, fish and chips, and my Moleskine.

On my second visit to the hotel the week before, the tall man with silver hair had been in the bar and greeted me, and we had swapped pleasantries. On this, my third visit, I was sitting at what was now "my table" by the wall near the front bay window, my pint and fish still untouched, pen in hand, feverish with concentration, when I sensed a presence. I looked up and there he was, standing over me with a quizzical but friendly smile. He was obviously a man of some breeding and, I guessed, some wealth. Hell, you could tell that from his shoes alone. He carried himself well. Not like those rich bankers who think they should have a big, fat, fucking bonus just for showing up for work in the morning and actually making it back to the office after a booze lunch. No; this guy had class. He had blue-gray, intelligent eyes and a round and somewhat handsome face. He was tall. I would always have to look up. A large man, not so much overweight as substantial. It was hard not to like him.

Still smiling, he asked, "You're an American?"

"Yes. Yes, I am," I said as pleasantly as I could, hoping this wasn't going to take too long, friendly guy or not. I had Chad Steel smelling madeleine sponge cake, traveling through a lawless, desolate section of the galaxy, thinking of home on the far side of nowhere.

"I thought so. I believe this is the third time you've visited us. Where are you staying? You're not staying with us." He said that last bit with a small laugh that was both good-natured and challenging.

"Renting a place in Silloth," I said matter-of-factly.

"I hope you don't mind me asking, but what are you doing in Silloth?" he said in a tone of voice that communicated both amazement and doubt, the subtext being, *Who the hell rents a place in Silloth?*

"I'm writing a novel."

"My goodness. A novelist! Do you mind?" And with that he sat down at my table. The big man reached across the table and engulfed my hand in his.

"Piers Cullingworth," he said.

"Drake. Drake Ramsey. Folks call me Drake."

And so we began.

Here's the short and skinny. You know his name: Piers Cullingworth. He was the manager and part-owner of the Skinburness Hotel, his partner being located in London. He was married with two kids. Jacklyn, his wife, also worked in the hotel, her specialty being "puddings." His word, not mine. Truth be told, she was a looker and I suspected she kept Piers on his toes. She didn't actually make pudding—you know, that soft, creamy stuff we eat with a spoon out of a bowl back in the States. She made cakes and pies, things the natives called "puddings." Desserts to us. Whatever.

Libbie was the younger of the two daughters, I guess around ten years old. Kara, the older, was about thirteen. They were both sharp as tacks and would grow up to be man-eaters. Glad I'll be an old fart when they begin to hunt. All in all, the Cullingworths were the best thing, along with the Tilfords, that could ever have happened to me in this far-flung outpost of wet, wind, and despair.

For whatever reason, the kids took to me. Have no idea why. I fell for them in short order. Kara would bring me my main meal, and later Libbie would saunter on over with my "pudding," as she put it. Jacklyn made damn good desserts, which saved me from further Allonby nightmares.

One of the real upsides of taking up residence in this desolate nowhere-town-of-lost-souls was meeting Piers and Basil for their prelunch walks. Basil was a large, blond, perpetually smiling dog. I'm talking a happy dog! Just between you and me, I never did get the name Basil. I mean, such an anal-retentive name for such a happy dog. Go figure the English. While Piers and I discussed life, the universe, and everything, focusing more than not on politics, Basil would enthusiastically chase a disgusting, saliva-soaked, dirty green tennis ball.

Piers and I were not exactly simpatico when it came to politics and the place of the 1 percent in the world. He actually thought the aristocracy were meant to rule. I did my best to set him straight on that, but it was a work in progress. He continued to argue passionately that he was a subject and not a citizen. I had to believe he was winding me up a little, partly because he was a damn good citizen, and partly because he liked winding me up. Having said that, he apparently loved the Queen and laughed when I told him the best thing for her and everyone else would be for her to find a damn job and stop living off the people. We met up most days, and even given our differences, we thought it was up to us to set the world right. We will continue to think this as long as we are still above ground.

There was one other person I need to tell you about, because he played a short but vital role in my story. A Spaniard by the name of Silvestre Tolentino. A short, round, middle-aged man with thick, shiny, black hair he combed straight back. I wouldn't want to call him ugly, but Brad Pitt he was not. As God is my witness, the ladies loved him. I don't know what he had, but if he could have bottled it, he would have been a rich man. Maybe it was his accent. Don't know. Shouldn't have cared. But I did.

Tolentino was Piers's assistant manager. He had a small apartment on the ground floor of the hotel's west wing, and it was a widely held secret that he rarely slept alone. I would watch the little guy in action, and on one particular night the green monster got ahold of my gut and twisted.

I was sitting at my table, minding my own business, drinking my second pint, and taking notes in my Moleskine. Chad Steel, a true space cowboy if ever there was one, had just encountered space pirates in the forbidden zone of Galaxy Quadrant Four along the Sagittarius Arm. Chad Steel was a long way from home, where he had dumped his girl before warping out of town. To say she was unworthy of Chad Steel is as obvious as the great black hole at the galaxy's center. And perhaps it was better that way. It's hard to love a rocket man whose fame is known in every bar and gin joint throughout the galaxy.

His ship, the *Liberté C57-D*, was a deep-space vessel flying out of the San Francisco Bay Area Cosmopolis, known by most everybody as the City. To say the *Liberté C57-D* flew out of the Cosmopolis of greater San Francisco is, of course, not literally true. She is a San Francisco Bay Area Cosmopolis project: funded with City money and crewed with City people. But she was built in Earth orbit, where function dominates form. She's equipped with the new warp engines developed at the Shanghai Metropolis Space Research and Development Center and is packed with all the technology and weapons you could dream up for space travel. When she returns home, she finds her rest in the City's docking space at Earth Orbiting Station Armstrong.

Chad Steel was just about to crank up those Shanghai warp engines and leave those pirates in his ion trail when I felt someone looking at me.

I looked up from my Moleskine, and sitting at the small table to the left of the bar was an African princess, maybe *the* African princess. At least that's what she looked like to me. Our eyes met briefly, and a whisper of a smile crossed her full, beautiful lips. But before I could turn that glance into an act of communication, Tolentino walked up to the table with his big, greasy smile. The African princess looked up and smiled back at him, and in that moment I had lost her. The little bastard.

Her natural hair fell to her shoulders. Her skin was night black and looked soft as velvet. Her eyes were mysterious and intelligent. Her body? Well, she actually made me nervous. What can I say? And oh, those lips.

Tolentino took her hand. As she bent over to stand, her pure white, low-cut dress, for only a split second, revealed her magnificent breasts. Her waist was thin, her hips perfect, and her legs were made to reduce a man to speechlessness. Hell, I blushed just looking at her, and as you know, I've been around a few very big blocks with any number of women. Just fact, no brag. I mean, it's who I am. But the African princess laid me low. Watching her leave the bar with Tolentino was downright maddening. Anyway, it was clear what Tolentino would be doing after work. I couldn't help thinking that it should have been me.

But here's where it gets interesting. Silvestre Tolentino was found dead on his bed the next morning.

5

That night after dinner I went over to Kelly and Parker Tilford's place. Kelly soon went up to bed, leaving Parker and me sitting in the living room drinking single malt. After a couple of those I was telling him all about Chad Steel and the madeleine sponge cake dilemma. Parker is a smart guy and talked for some time about the profundity that is Proust. All I could think was that throughout my six months of reading Proust, I had been profoundly bored. However, by the time he meandered his way back to Chad Steel, we decided my space adventurer needed an appropriate backstory. You get it, right? What book, and hopefully movie, is worth its weight without a good backstory to enable the psychological exploration of the main protagonist? I mean, how boring is a protagonist who doesn't have a dead kid or alcoholic wife or a father who beat him? Though let's be honest: it would take a foolish man, even a father, to beat Chad Steel.

Suddenly Parker got up, saying he had just the thing to help us ease our way into Chad Steel's life. He went into the kitchen, and I heard him open the freezer compartment of the fridge. I could hear him rummaging around, and then he started yelling for Kelly to come to the kitchen. I got up to see what was going on. Parker was asking Kelly, in her PJs, what happened to his grass, more than a little too loud. With the straightest face you can imagine, she denied flushing it down the toilet. Parker and I went back to the living room and had to settle for the whisky.

By the time I got to bed, I couldn't sleep for worrying about Chad Steel's backstory. I sat up in bed with my Moleskine, jotting down ideas until four in the morning. I did nail it, however. Chad Steel's trauma as a child was having too many areas in which he could excel, given his extreme intelligence and physical prowess. Should he go into medicine and heal the masses? Into politics to bring prosperity and liberty to all human-occupied planets? Or should he become a philosopher and solve the great mysteries of human existence? In the end, he could only free himself from the oppression of excellence by traveling to the stars in the *Liberté C57-D*.

Good, don't you think? I mean, yes, I have to spend the right amount of time with the young Chad Steel agonizing over his future. And I guess if I'm going to stick to my Proustian ambitions, I will have to write two hundred pages about the night young Chad Steel decided politics was absolutely not worthy of his time and intelligence.

With a peaceful mind I fell asleep but was rudely awakened when Kara and Libbie called me at ten o'clock the next morning. In hushed but excited voices, they said, "Someone killed Silvestre! You've got to come right away!"

Always the reporter, my first thought was murder. With the

knowledge that Chad Steel's backstory was established, I got up, showered, and dressed in record time, despite my single-malt-soaked liver. When I arrived at the hotel, the girls were outside waiting for me. Basil was there too, with his big dog smile. But it was clear that the death of Silvestre Tolentino had hit the girls hard. They had been crying. They each took a hand and ushered me through the back entrance to the family apartment, Basil leading the way. Jacklyn was making coffee in the kitchen.

"Drake! Thank God you're here," she said, handing me a cup of joe.

"I came as soon as I heard. Where's Piers?" I asked, taking a sip.

"He's with the police," said Kara.

"I'll take you to him. You girls stay here. Basil, you stay with them," Jacklyn said.

When we got to Tolentino's apartment, Jacklyn said she didn't want to see the body, so I went in without her. I found Piers standing with the cops outside Tolentino's bedroom door. It was open, so I looked in. The cops saw me looking at the dead man and asked who I was.

"He's a friend. I called him to come by and, well, help us get through this," Piers said to the number one cop, the one doing all the talking. I shot Piers a quick glance. We both knew that he hadn't called me and that he certainly didn't need help to cope. Something else was up.

"Hello, Inspector. My name is Drake Ramsey. People call me Drake. Do you mind if I look around while you guys talk?"

"Well, yes, I do, Mr. Ramsey."

"Please, Inspector. Mr. Ramsey is a friend and not a little inexperienced in these matters. I would consider it a personal favor if you would allow Mr. Ramsey to have a look around," Piers said with considerable gravitas.

"Okay, but don't touch anything," said the cop, looking slightly uneasy.

"No problem."

I quickly clicked into my reporter mode. No forced entry. The front door to the apartment was undamaged, but the inside chain had been cut with bolt cutters. Obviously, at some point Piers, or someone else, had used a house key and found the door chained. Instead of ripping the chain off the door frame, the person cut the damn thing. Smart.

In the living room, on the table in front of the couch, there were two wineglasses and two bottles of red wine, one empty and one half full. The couch cushions were flattened, and it didn't take a lot of imagination to figure out why. No doubt the African princess liked red wine. The overhead light and one floor lamp were on.

I made my way to the adjoining kitchen. A cutting board sitting next to the sink showed the remnants of crackers and cheese. Otherwise the place was spit-polished clean. The light was on.

I walked down the hall to the bedroom. The hall light was on. It was a nice bedroom and bigger than I would have guessed. There was a double bed with bedside tables on each side, each with a lamp. There was a large window to the left as I entered the room. Under the window was a desk and chair. On the desk was a laptop, pens and pencils in a mug, a pad, and a picture of a woman and child. And oh, a desk lamp. To the right of the bed was a built-in closet, and there was a small but comfortable chair in the corner with a round table and floor lamp. On the table was a wineglass. There was some white wine in the glass. Next to the glass was a paperback copy of *Fifty Shades of Grey*.

The drawer of the bedside table, the one between the bed and the desk, was open, and a ripped condom packet was on the tabletop. I looked in the drawer and saw nothing unusual, though his supply of condoms was more than I could use in a year. I was about to go rooting through the drawer but thought better of it.

I suddenly noticed that the desk lamp, both bedside table lamps, and the floor lamp next to the chair were all on. The whole damn apartment was lit up like Broadway at Christmas.

To that point I had avoided looking at the body itself, but the time had come. Tolentino was lying on top of the bedcovers, the bed never having been turned down, the pillows still tucked in place. He was completely naked, flat on his back, his arms at his side. His legs were only slightly parted. He had a round belly and the beginnings of a nice pair of man-boobs. Definitely too much hair. He was drained of all color. Looked like a freaking ghost, and I'm not talking about fucking Casper-the-friendly. His eyes were wide open, staring at the ceiling. His mouth was opened wide as well. Too wide.

I leaned over to take a closer look at dead Silvestre Tolentino lying there in his birthday suit. There were no obvious marks on the body, but upon closer examination I did see a small cut on his left cheek. It didn't look like he nicked himself shaving. Too deep for that. And as it turned out, he wasn't completely naked. There was a condom on his limp penis that I hadn't noticed, for obvious reasons. But what was most striking was that he looked like he had been frightened to death. It was not a pleasant sight. The whole damn thing was pretty creepy.

Bottom line, all the windows were shut tight and locked. There was no sign of a struggle, except for the action on the couch, though I wouldn't call that a struggle. The apartment was clean and everything was in its place. Job done, I turned my attention back to the cops and Piers.

"Mr. Cullingworth, it looks like a heart attack or a stroke or something. As you said, the door was locked, and he was in here alone," said the talkative one.

"What about the wineglasses?" I asked quietly.

Piers turned to me and said, "Paul, one of our waiters, saw Miss Zuri Manyika enter the flat with Silvestre about one in the morning. I assume she and Silvestre shared the wine." He turned to the cop and continued, "No one saw her leave, which is no surprise. We had finished for the night, and the staff had gone home."

So the African princess has a name. Zuri Manyika, I thought.

"Well, she obviously left," said the cop. "The door was locked, and she wasn't here in the morning when you entered the flat."

"Shouldn't she be questioned anyway? I mean, just in case it wasn't a heart attack?" I said a little more forcefully. I was guessing these cops came from the small town of Wigton down the road and hadn't had too many murder cases to deal with. I was thinking, *Okay. It looks like natural causes, but what about that damn condom? And all the lights? And the glass of white wine in the bedroom? Who was drinking that?*

"We'll need to speak with Miss Manyika. But there's no indication that anything untoward happened here," said number one cop.

"What about the condom?" I asked.

"What about it?" It was number two cop. "You know what a condom is for, don't you, Mr. Ramsey?" Number two could talk and was a bit of a wiseass. "I don't see any reason to embarrass this Miss Manyika with questions about a condom."

"It's empty. It's clean. Never been used. Go look." Both cops turned their heads and looked reluctantly at the body on the bed.

"What? What are you talking about?" said cop number two, showing a bit of his dark side.

"Inspectors, why was he lying on *top* of his bed, not *in* the bed, with a condom that he never used on his penis? I doubt he showed Zuri Manyika to the door, got naked, put a condom on, and then stretched out on his bed to have a heart attack. And why the second condom if no one was with him, assuming he and Zuri Manyika did it on the couch before she left? Most men don't masturbate with a condom. And would you masturbate after having had sex with Zuri Manyika? I mean, come on! It seems more like someone led him to the bed, where he put on the condom to have sex for a second time that night, and then … well, then what? And besides, look at his face. It's creepy. And every damn light in the apartment is on. He wasn't on his way to bed to sleep," I said.

Throughout my observations, Piers was looking uncomfortable. Something was bothering him, and I needed to get him alone.

"Mr. Cullingworth, do you know Miss Manyika?" Number one cop was back in control.

"Not well, but a little. She's a guest in the hotel. I've only talked to her a few times. She's a very friendly young woman. She is originally from Zimbabwe but moved to America when she was a girl. She's now an American citizen, currently living in New Orleans. She has a cousin in London, and she made her reservation from there, I think about two weeks ago. She's here on her own and doesn't venture far from the hotel. She uses the gym every day, if that helps."

"Right, we'll talk to her."

"Please don't upset her any more than necessary."

"Bill, you stay here with the body until the coroner comes. Stay until she takes it away." So number two cop had a name.

And with that, the other cop and I followed Piers out of the apartment to reception, where he asked Lily Henderson, a good Glasgow girl working behind the desk, for Zuri Manyika's room number. On the way up the stairs to the guest rooms, I couldn't help thinking that Lily Henderson looked more than a little distressed. I'm sure she had been crying for Silvestre Tolentino.

6

P iers had been knocking on the door for some time, and number one cop, whose name turned out to be Ralph Witherspoon, was getting antsy. "Mr. Cullingworth, I assume you have a key to this door," said Inspector Witherspoon.

Piers looked uneasy and Witherspoon added quickly, "Look. Mr. Tolentino is dead and Miss Manyika may be involved. We need to check to see if she is safe."

So what happened to "natural causes"? Inspector Witherspoon was capable of changing his position fairly quickly. Good to know.

"Inspector, the Do Not Disturb sign is on the door. I can't just open a guest's room and go snooping around," said Piers.

"I will take full responsibility. Now, please," Inspector Witherspoon said in his most policemanlike tone.

Piers reached into his pocket for the master key, and just as he was about to insert it into the door lock, we heard the safety chain on the other side of the door slide. We each took a step back.

The door opened and there stood Zuri Manyika. Her hair was disheveled and her eyes were half-closed with sleep. She was barefoot. Her toenails were painted with red polish so dark it almost looked like blood. She wore a Skinburness Hotel robe loosely tied around her waist—her neck, her chest, and a hint of her breasts visible. It was clear her appearance had nothing to do with whoever she might find when she opened the door, but all to do with not giving a damn. Her right hand was in the pocket of the robe, obviously holding something.

She looked at us for a moment, clearly annoyed. "What? I was sleeping," she said, as cold as a Valley Forge winter.

We stood there looking at her, saying nothing. "What?" she said loudly to Piers.

"Miss Manyika, I'm sorry to bother you, but we've got a problem, and the inspector here needs to speak with you," Piers said as politely as possible.

"Oh, God. Seriously?" Zuri Manyika said absentmindedly, looking down at her chest and realizing how much of her assets were on show. She let go of the object in the robe pocket and pulled the robe tight with both hands. Whatever was in the pocket was obviously heavy, pulling it out of shape. As soon as she was nicely covered up, she put her hand back in the pocket. My trained eye and all my experience on the *Fremont Argus News* demanded I ask myself a simple question: *Is she packing?* But standing so close to her for the first time, I could only confirm that, yes, her skin was soft as velvet. The question of steel heat in her robe pocket dissolved before my imagination.

"Yes, seriously, Miss Manyika. I want to speak to you as soon as possible," said Inspector Witherspoon.

"What's this about?"

"We'll discuss that during the interview."

"Okay, okay. Can I at least shower and dress?"

"Of course," said Piers. "When you're ready, why don't you come down to my office? The receptionist will show you the way."

"I'll see you in your office in forty-five minutes. Is that okay?" she said to Piers. She paused, looked me in the eyes for a fraction of a second, and then closed the door. She was beautiful!

Witherspoon said he was going to check on PC Bill Jamison (I registered the police constable's last name) and afterward would meet us in the office. Piers and I went to the kitchen, grabbed some coffee, and went to his office.

The office was spacious, with a large window looking out on a small garden in between the two wings of the hotel. In the garden were tables and chairs for the guests, though they'd need a good clean before anyone could use them. The office itself had a large desk with a high-backed leather desk chair. To the right of the desk was a small bookshelf. Hanging above the bookshelf were pictures of the hotel at various periods of its existence. To the left were three comfortable chairs surrounding a low, round table. The office is lushly carpeted in a deep, rich cranberry color. We sat in two of the chairs by the low table. Above our heads was a large Lake District painting by a local artist. That's local to the Lake District, mind you. I suspect the natives in this Cut-It-Off-Mummy-Town on the Solway would have neither the skill nor inclination to paint anything other than a wall.

"Something's bothering you, Piers. Spill," I said.

"This isn't the first death in the hotel. There have been eleven other deaths since the hotel opened," Piers said.

"Twelve! You're kidding. When was it opened?"

"Not so loud!" Piers warned me. "Around 1885. The exact date isn't really known, but 1885 is good enough."

"That's about one death every ten and a half years. Why the hell wasn't this place closed down?"

"People die. Hotels have a lot of people passing through them."

"The police …?"

"The police have never had any suspicions."

"But still … There's something else. Something about these deaths and Silvestre's death," I pressed.

"Most of the deaths occurred in the Edwin Hodge Banks West Wing. It's always been rumored that—"

Just then Inspector Witherspoon knocked, opened the door, and walked in.

Piers asked Lily Henderson to bring in a pot of coffee and four cups. Witherspoon informed us that PC Jamison was accompanying the body to Carlisle with the coroner, where she would do her thing. And before we knew it, Zuri Manyika was being shown into the office. Lily Henderson looked at Inspector Witherspoon uneasily and then left.

7

Zuri Manyika sat between Witherspoon and me, while Piers brought his chair from around the desk. Coffee was poured, and a few obligatory comments were made about the shitty weather, which Witherspoon bet Zuri Manyika didn't get in New Orleans. Ha ha ha. That sort of thing.

Zuri Manyika was all polished and shining. This time I was pretty damn sure she did care who was looking at her. She wore a snug light-blue dress short enough to show off her wraparound legs. She wore makeup, but only lightly. As she sipped her coffee, she looked over her cup as if asking when we were going to begin in earnest.

"Miss Manyika ..." Piers began.

"You can call me Zuri if you like. I don't mind," she said softly. Her change in mood was so striking that I sat back in my chair. No one could ever accuse her of being stupid, and certainly not naive. She was working it, or rather us.

"Thank you … Zuri. Last night—"

Piers was interrupted again, this time by Inspector Witherspoon. "If I may, Mr. Cullingworth," said the good inspector. Piers shot him a look but immediately deferred to him. "Miss Manyika, I understand you visited Mr. Tolentino in his flat last night. Is that correct?"

"Yes, I did, though I'm not sure it's any of your business. Why do you ask?" she said, slowly placing her cup in the saucer on the table, then sitting back with her hands in her lap. We were all sitting back in our chairs, our bodies anticipating the long haul. All except Inspector Witherspoon, who sat in the middle of his chair, straight-backed, with a notebook on his knees.

"I think it's best I ask the questions here. Let's get right to the point," said Witherspoon. "Ah, Miss Manyika, did you, ah, have intimacies with Mr. Tolentino?"

If Zuri was surprised by the question, she hid it well. Without hesitating or showing any embarrassment, she said, "Yes, Inspector. I had two glasses of wine and one intimacy with Mr. Tolentino."

"Forgive me for asking. Did you and Mr. Tolentino use protection?"

"Yes, Inspector. No protection, no intimacy, as I'm sure you will understand," she said, never taking her eyes off Witherspoon.

"You said, and again I'm sorry, you had one intimacy with Mr. Tolentino?"

"That's right. One."

"So that would be one condom …" Speaking to himself while writing in his notebook. "Ah, and this really is awkward. Did Mr. Tolentino come to completion during your intimacy?"

Zuri Manyika smiled at this question, as did I. I suspect Piers was also laughing inside but would never show it.

"Yes Inspector, Mr. Tolentino certainly did 'come to completion,' as you put it. Yes, I would describe it as coming to completion. Yes, he did."

"I assume he disposed of the condom after completion?" Inspector Witherspoon asked, not looking at Zuri but writing in his notebook. I did wonder what happened in the good inspector's bed with Mrs. Inspector. Completion, or not, was the $64,000 question.

Zuri remained silent, just looking at Inspector Witherspoon. No one spoke for a moment. Then she said, "You really want me to tell you what he did with a used condom?"

"Yes, ma'am, if you could, please."

"He got off me. He sat on the edge of the couch. He took the condom off. He got up and walked to the bathroom, where I assume he flushed it down the toilet. Which I think is not uncommon, Inspector. Did you get that, or do you want me to repeat it?"

I do believe I saw another smile cross her lips.

"Thank you, no, I got that. No need to repeat it. Did he then put another, a second, condom on?"

"Now why the hell would he do that? I told you, we did it once and then I left."

"And what time would that have been?"

Zuri sighed, some annoyance creeping in. No one had yet acknowledged that Tolentino was actually dead. Did she know? Was she playing us? I honestly couldn't tell. Was I losing my touch, being away from *Fremont Argus News* too long? Or was it her perfume, that did what all perfumes were supposed to do, only better? (For the record, a whole hell of a lot better.)

"I left Silvestre about two forty-five in the morning. I went back to my room, showered, and went to bed by three fifteen. I know because I saw the time when I turned the bedside clock around. The red light of the numbers bothers me. Now, why don't you tell me what is going on?"

Piers and Witherspoon looked at each other, but I kept my eyes on Zuri. My God, her lips were made for kissing. No matter what name you threw at God.

"Well, Miss Manyika, I'm afraid I have some bad news. Mr. Tolentino was found dead in his bed this morning," Inspector Witherspoon said.

"Actually, he was found dead *on* his bed, not in it," I said, looking at Zuri. Witherspoon glanced at me with annoyance.

Zuri didn't say anything, but fear—yes, I was sure it was fear—flashed across her face. She turned to me and said, "How did he die?"

"Well, now, that's the question," I said.

"And what does this have to do with me?" she said, still looking at me.

"It is possible you were the last person to see Mr. Tolentino alive," said Inspector Witherspoon. "And to answer your first question, we don't yet know how he died. We will have to wait for the coroner's report, which I imagine won't take long. We don't get many unusual deaths in these parts."

"Unusual. How do you mean unusual?" she asked, her voice less assured.

"Miss Manyika, I hope you are not checking out of the hotel anytime soon," said Inspector Witherspoon, no longer hiding in his notebook. He was finding his voice.

"Actually, I was going to ask Mr. Cullingworth if I could stay a bit longer."

"And why is that, if I may ask?" said Cumbria's finest.

"For personal reasons. I need more time to, well, rest and unwind, and the Skinburness Hotel is a quiet and comfortable place to do that."

"Thank you, Miss Manyika. There will—"

Inspector Witherspoon cut Piers off again in midsentence.

Though I had not known Piers long, I nonetheless knew him well and could tell his patience was running very thin. As I said, Piers was a nice guy, but I had seen him angry, and no one wanted to be on the other end of that shit storm. Not even a country cop.

"Not much to do around here, Miss Manyika. I mean, some would say the Skinburness is even a bit isolated. Why here?" asked Inspector Witherspoon, perhaps getting a bit too much into his role.

"It's quiet, Inspector. I like quiet. The leisure center is well equipped, and I like walking along the waterfront. The food is excellent. There's a decent library. The staff is friendly and efficient. Can't you understand why a person who needs rest would appreciate a hotel like this?" She looked at Witherspoon and then to Piers.

"There is no problem with your staying with us longer. Stay as long as you like," said Piers. "And thank you for the kind words."

"Okay then," said Inspector Witherspoon as he closed his notebook and stood up. "I think we're done here. Thank you, Miss Manyika. And you too, Mr. Cullingworth. Mr. Ramsey, I suspect I'll be seeing you again."

"Count on it." I smiled.

"Mr. Cullingworth, could you ensure that Mr. Tolentino's flat remains untouched and locked up tight? Thank you." And with that, Witherspoon turned to leave.

"Inspector Witherspoon," Zuri said, "my name is *Ms.* Manyika." Witherspoon paused, looking at Zuri, and then left the room.

Zuri stood up and, turning to me, said, "Mr. Ramsey, is it? I'm here on my own for the time being, and while I want quiet and rest, I do enjoy conversation. Perhaps we could have lunch or dinner sometime." She smiled.

"Ah, of course. That would be great. And it's Drake. Folks call me Drake. Let me give you my number," I said. I walked to Piers's desk, found a piece of paper and a pen, and jotted down my cell number. "Here, and I must say, that's an enticing perfume." That last bit about the perfume was a little bold, I guess, but what the hell. I had nothing to lose. And hey, sometimes you've gotta grab life by the tail. I'm just saying.

"Thank you, Drake. I don't have my phone with me, but when I get back to the room, I'll text you. And thanks, but I'm not wearing perfume." She smiled at me and then turned to Piers. "Mr. Cullingworth, I'm very sorry to hear about Silvestre. He will be hard to replace. And thank you for letting me stay longer in your wonderful hotel." She smiled again. Not the same smile she had flashed my way, I hasten to add. "Gentlemen …" she said and left the office.

Piers and I looked at each other, and he said, "Careful there, mate."

8

Before I could respond to Piers's warning, the door opened. It was Jacklyn. She looked stressed but also in control. It didn't take long to learn that Jacklyn was good in a crisis and could be counted on. "The girls and I have prepared lunch, if you're hungry. And I've checked to make sure we're all set for the lunch crowd. You've got time. Come to the kitchen and eat and fill me in."

It was a large kitchen for a hotel apartment, and it functioned as both a food preparation space and a dining area. We all sat around the table with sandwiches and a large salad. I found myself in between Kara and Libbie, which wasn't a bad place to be. Basil sat by Libbie's side, looking up at the table. The rain was pounding the kitchen window. I had no idea when it had started, but it fit the mood. I hadn't known Tolentino that well and, to be honest, hadn't found him best bud material. But the Cullingworths had liked him and worked with him, and they all were thrown off-center.

Piers recapped the events of the morning, leaving out the nakedness and the limp, condom-covered penis. Seemed only right, but I had little doubt Libbie and Kara could have handled the details. Nonetheless, he didn't overkill on the nature of Tolentino's death, only saying they'd have to wait for the coroner's report. At that, the two girls leaned forward over the table and looked across me at each other. There was definitely something in the air, something wanting to spark. It was Libbie who lit the match.

"It's the ghost," Libbie said confidently.

"Ghost!" I almost shouted. "What ghost? I've never heard about a ghost."

"Libbie, this is not the time," her father said, not kindly.

"She's right, you know. Silvestre lived in the west wing. All the deaths were in the west wing," Kara said.

I suddenly replayed the telephone call from Libbie that started this bleak day. She had said, "Someone *killed* Silvestre," because that's what she believed. That's what got murder into my head, but I hadn't figured the murderer was a ghost. What crap.

"Okay. Reality check," I said more calmly. "There is no such thing as ghosts."

"Well, Drake," Jacklyn said, "hate to shake your reality, but I've seen her."

"Her. The ghost is a her?" I asked, and then said, "Have you kids seen this ghost? I mean, come on."

"No, we haven't, but Mum has, and everybody knows there's a ghost in the west wing," said Libbie.

"You guys have been in Silloth too long," I said. "There's no such thing as ghosts."

"Okay, let's all calm down. This is nonsense and you all know it," Piers said, holding up his hand to cut off Libbie's protest. "It's all nonsense. Just stories people love to tell about big old hotels."

"So how did Silvestre die?" Kara asked.

"I don't know. We have to wait to hear from the coroner," Piers answered.

"You're not going to tell us, are you?" Libbie asked.

"Probably not," said Piers.

"You know we'll just hear about it anyway," said Kara, joining in. Basil thumped his tail and sighed.

"Piers, have you seen Lily lately?" said Jacklyn, changing the subject. "She's been crying and is really upset."

"Just when she brought us coffee. Should I check in with her, do you think?"

"I think it would be a good idea. She seems to be taking Silvestre's death harder than the rest of the staff," said Jacklyn.

"Well, that's no surprise. Everybody knows she and Silvestre—" Libbie said, but was cut off by Jacklyn.

"Enough. You don't know a thing," Jacklyn said, getting up from the table.

The conversation ended when Jacklyn brought out ice cream, thankfully not Allonby ice cream. I decided I needed to get back home, take a walk when the rain stopped and the wind died down. Clear my head of nonsense. But I was intrigued by Lily Henderson. As Piers was walking me to the front door, he said, "Obviously, it's not ghosts that concern me. It is adding another death to the hotel's folklore. Our reputation doesn't need this. It's business I'm worried about. These are hard times, and the government's austerity program isn't helping. Silvestre was a colleague and friend, but the Skinburness Hotel is a challenge, and his death doesn't help. I'll need to get onto the agency today about a new deputy. Silvestre will be hard to replace."

We stopped beside the open front door. I hadn't just fallen off the turnip truck. I knew Piers hadn't spilled, at least not entirely.

I said, "There's something you're not telling me. Something about Silvestre? About his death?"

Piers hesitated and then said quietly, "This goes no further." I nodded. "He had some pretty big gambling debts. He confided in me about a month ago; well, actually he asked me for a loan. I refused. I honestly don't know the details and didn't want to know them. But it sounded too shady to be healthy."

"You thinking mob crap?"

"I have no idea. Besides, the flat was locked up tight. He didn't let anyone in."

I didn't know what to say, so we just stared at each other for a few moments. Then I slapped him on the arm and turned to leave.

"Wait. One more thing," I said, turning back to Piers. "What's the deal with this Lily Henderson? Something up there?"

"Poor Lily," Piers said with a little laugh. "Lily first came to Silloth for the Glasgow Fortnight."

"The what?" I asked.

"Glasgow Fortnight. Each August the Lido fills up with people from Glasgow who come down for a two-week holiday."

The natives call two weeks a "fortnight." Quaint.

"Lily came down with her family, and one afternoon she and some friends came to the hotel for lunch. Kind of unusual. The Glasgow crowds tend to stick to the Lido. But she came back a few times, and one thing led to another, and I offered her a job covering the front desk."

Piers paused, smiled, and then continued. "I'm fairly sure she and Silvestre had a regular thing going. Actually, I did wonder if maybe she had fallen in love with him, which wouldn't have been the smartest thing she ever did. Anyway, I'll talk to her. Not to worry." And with that, we parted.

That night I had dinner with Kelly and Parker. It was becoming something of a routine. I didn't fight it. The food was on the table and the wine was poured before the topic of Silvestre Tolentino's death came up. But as sure as the rain falls down on this Graytown-on-the-Solway, it did. Nothing gets by Kelly, and the death was all over town. So I told them the story, including the naked body and protected penis. Parker tagged it *The Mysterious Case of the Limp Penis*.

"*The Mysterious Case of the Limp Penis* is a typical locked-room mystery," Parker said with a sly smile. "Once we determine what is impossible, what remains can only be the truth, no matter how improbable. It all started with Poe's 'The Murders in the Rue Morgue.' Monsieur Dupin discovered that the windows had spring devices that could be manipulated. Do the windows in the Skinburness have spring devices?"

"Not that I've seen. Everything was locked up tight, all the lights were on, and poor Tolentino was lying there as naked as a jaybird. But you're right. I should have a closer look, without the cops looking over my shoulder trying to see what I'm up to," I said.

We batted around some ideas, assuming it was murder, of course. At one point I asked about the other deaths in the hotel's history, and for once Kelly was not an ever-flowing fountain of information. As we sat there, I thought, *These other deaths are important. Don't know why. Just gut-talk. I better go with it. That's what I do. Hell, that's what broke the parking lot scandal. Gut-talk.*

I told Parker and Kelly that it would be good to find out about the other deaths and quick, and then bitched that on the *Fremont Argus News* I had an intern to do this kind of legwork, or, more accurately, computer work. Hell, I even had an intern on the *Union City Gazette.*

"I could be your intern. For a price, of course," Kelly said, filling my glass with more red.

"She's good," Parker said, getting up to find the single malt.

I wondered for a minute what my dear grandmother would think about the way I was spending her money. But I had to admit Kelly seemed to know everything going on, and I would have bet she was on a first-name basis with every soul in Cumbria. We played at haggling over her fee, me pointing out that on the *Fremont Argus News* and the *Union City Gazette*, my interns worked for free, Kelly emphasizing that I didn't know shit about Cumbria or the Skinburness Hotel and if I wanted to write that novel I kept talking about, I'd need help. Kelly was rarely wrong. The amount agreed was not much more than a token. Truth was, Kelly wanted to play. Parker found it amusing.

We agreed she'd get to work on the deaths first thing in the morning: names, ages, dates, nationalities, that sort of thing. As many details as she could find. Me? Well, if Chad Steel was going to make my fortune, then I would have to refocus and stop thinking about ghosts and the full lips and black velvet skin of the African princess.

Regarding Tolentino's gambling problems and the possible mob intrigue, I said not a word. Nor did I mention Lily Henderson, a Glasgow girl who had fallen hard for a Spaniard who liked the ladies—apparently all the ladies.

It was a cold night, so I lit the gas heater in my study when I got home and sat at the small desk facing a blank wall. I wasn't totally convinced that the gas heater wouldn't one day kill me. The study was a small room with a desk, desk chair, of course, and a lounge chair. Next to the large chair was a floor lamp for reading. There was also an overhead light and a desk lamp. The walls were a dingy off-white. They needed painting. Hell, all the walls in that place needed painting. The room had only one small window facing the back garden and the garbage cans. The natives called them "bins." There was nothing on the walls. Six months wasn't enough time to go looking for art.

I cracked open a brand-new bottle of Macallan single malt and practiced staring at my laptop. It was at times like these I wished I smoked cigars or a pipe. It took thirty minutes, but as I poured my second Macallan, it became clear that Chad Steel needed a girl. A hot girl.

I had him space-dock the *Liberté C57-D* for routine maintenance and refueling over a small planet in the Crux-Scutum inner galactic arm near Centaurus, a long way from the Orion Arm that held his home planet. He and his motley crew of ten shuttled down to the surface for much needed R&R. It was the second day on-planet when he saw her across a crowded outdoor market. The weather was gray and wet, but her beauty shone through. He instantly forgot all about the woman he had dumped back home. Couldn't even remember her name. If it wasn't love at first sight there in the Crux-Scutum Arm, it certainly had to be something. As he started walking toward her through the crowd, he thought, *Better living through chemicals.*

She was blue. She was clearly not a native of this windswept, gray, wet world where the people walked with bent shoulders and eyes fixed on the ground. Her beauty could never in the life of a billion suns have been born of that place. And I must add, she was emphatically not that absurdly hideous blue of the Na'vi. What was Cameron thinking? Fucking Smurfs! Most of the damn movie looks like a big cartoon. No; she was a gentle, morning-sky blue, and humanoid all the way. Suddenly it hit me. My working title for the novel would be *The Woman in Blue Skies.* Her name was Rashida.

Okay. I admit, approaching a blue woman in a filthy, muddy, dripping wet market filled with beings from numerous planets and species is not like strolling with Mme. Swann in the Allée de la Reine Marguerite. But in my defense, my book is Proustian-like, not a freakin' copy. Besides, Chad Steel has his own kind of romance. He doesn't spend six volumes moaning about love and life. Chad

Steel loves and lives *now* because you never know what tomorrow will bring.

There are two things you need to know about Rashida. First, when she saw Chad Steel approaching her, she was instantly drawn to him. Of course, she was her own person, intelligent and strong. After all, she had been wandering through the inner galaxy on her own at the time she encountered Chad Steel. Still, she practically threw herself in his arms, metaphorically speaking. Literal throwing would come a few hours later when they found a small but dry room in an inconspicuous inn. In no time their beautiful bodies were intertwined in the swirling passion of sex. As it would turn out, on all the seventeen billion earthlike planets in the galaxy, Chad Steel was the only man who could make Rashida blush, which in her case meant turning a slightly deeper blue. Second thing you should know: Rashida was always packing heat on her right hip, and on her left, hidden steel.

9

In the morning I walked into Winters Newsagents on Eden Street to see if any of the local rags had picked up on Tolentino's unfortunate departure, and I came home with the *News & Star* and the *Cumberland News*. When I moved into this tall and narrow house, I had planted a coffeemaker and grounds on the small table by the window in my study to save a million trips up and down the stairs to the kitchen. I brewed a pot and then took the papers and my cup of java to the living room. I sat in the chair in the bay window and began my search.

As it turned out, both the *News & Star* and the *Cumberland News* had short mentions of the death, but only the *News & Star* linked Tolentino's demise to the other past deaths in the hotel. Unfortunately for Kelly, the *News & Star* story was lacking in details, precision, and depth. Obviously written by some hack. My God, where was the pride in the trade? And where was Woodward when you needed him? I did discover, however, that Tolentino was originally from Madrid, where an ex-wife and daughter still lived. As I said, I was not particularly impressed with Tolentino, but death usually leaves someone behind, and that is sad.

I lingered too long over my java, searching the papers for other news, any news, to be found amongst the adverts. I mean, last night I had left Rashida with her sky-blue perfect legs wrapped around Chad Steel's head. I thought I should get back to it, but after a couple more cups I decided to head down to the Skinburness instead to see what was up.

As I stood beside my red shitmobile trying to decide whether to drive or walk, I noticed—how could I not—that the big black birds in the stand of trees were particularly loud, no doubt preparing to drop their dirty on my car. I decided to drive. I drove slowly down the road toward Skinburness. The wind was picking up and there was white water on the Solway. To my right were bungalows, all in a row, pretty much all the same. The bent old vicar lived in one of those boxes, though which one I did not know.

As I pulled into the parking lot, Piers and Basil were coming out of the back door for their prelunch walk. Understandably, Piers was in a somber and reflective mood on this, the morning after. No time for the exploits of prime ministers and presidents: our conversation was all about Silvestre Tolentino. This is what I learned.

Inspector Witherspoon and PC Jamison had been back to the hotel in the morning to question staff and hotel guests and conduct a thorough check of Tolentino's apartment. Somewhat disturbing to me was the news that a sleepless guest, wandering around the hotel in the early hours looking for the library, had heard a loud argument coming from Tolentino's apartment at about two forty-five. Piers didn't have to tell me that the first thing Inspector Witherspoon wanted to do was interview Zuri again. Unfortunately, she was nowhere to be found, and the good inspector had failed to get her cell phone number the day before. I wasn't about to give it to him.

As we walked along, now in a light drizzle, I remained silent, absorbing the fact that Zuri had in effect lied to us, albeit through omission. But a lie nonetheless. When you are being questioned by the cops over a mysterious death, you need a damn good reason not to mention a little thing like a fight. I was willing to bet she had a good reason; I just didn't know if it would prove to be good news or bad. I decided to make it my business to find her before the Wigton law dogs did.

"Piers," I said finally, "I'd like to have a look at the apartment again, without the cops looking over my shoulder."

"Is that a good idea? The place is taped off."

"You've got the key. I won't disturb anything. I'm willing to bet Silvestre didn't die of natural causes."

"Based on what?"

"On my gut," I said, as Piers had a little grunt of a laugh. I wasn't offended.

Ever since Parker had made the joke about the locked-room mystery, I couldn't get Hercule Poirot out of my mind. Kaitlyn Lethbridge had a secret addiction to Agatha Christie's Poirot, and last Christmas we'd watched *Hercule Poirot's Christmas* on TV. In that story, there is a family sitting around at Christmas, and they hear a crash and then a scream coming from the father's study. They break down the door and find the old man murdered. He is alone in the room and all the windows are locked. Well, one is locked and one is permanently frozen a few inches open. If I remember correctly, and I usually do, the killer goes into the room, kills the vic, piles pieces of furniture on top of each other, ties a thin cord around the bottom piece of furniture, probably a chair, and then hangs the cord out that partially opened window. He leaves the room and locks the door from the outside. Later he goes around the house and pulls the cord, and wham-bam thank-you-ma'am, a loud crash. People break down the door and find furniture all over the place and assume there must have been a struggle. Oh yeah, there was also something about a recorded scream. You get the idea. The point is, there's always an answer to the locked-room mystery.

There had to have been something like that going on in Tolentino's apartment, and I had to find it. If it weren't for the door chain being on, it could have been a stolen key or God knew what. But that damn door chain bothered me.

When we got back to the hotel and the Cullingworths' apartment, Basil headed for the kitchen. Piers handed me Tolentino's key and then went to clean up for work. I limboed low under the yellow tape across the door and closed and locked the door behind me. Now alone, I took my time looking around. The apartment was nicely furnished, not inexpensively. The artwork and photographs on the walls were originals. There was a coat closet immediately to the right of the entrance. I opened the door to have a look inside, something I had been unable to do when the cops were there. No surprises, just a couple of coats on hangers, a hat, and gloves on a shelf.

I stepped out of the closet and looked again at the sofa, the empty wineglasses, the crushed pillows. I thought, *Lucky bastard.*

After a wasted moment imagining Tolentino's good fortune, I set about examining the windows, hoping to find old-fashioned latches. No such luck. All the windows were double glazed, as the natives say, and actually looked kind of new. Worse still, each window had key lock handles, and every one of them was locked up tight. Two windows in the living room, one large one in the kitchen, and two in the bedroom. All locked. The keys to the windows were easy to find. I just searched cabinets and drawers in each room.

I looked for other means of entering and exiting the apartment, but could find none. No vents, no closets with false walls. No nothing. The damn place was sealed.

I had to admit Silvestre Tolentino had a nice bolt-hole here. Interesting DVD library and even a few books. His multimedia center had cost him a very pretty dime, by the looks of it. The liquor cabinet was well stocked, as was the wine rack in the kitchen. I went through his closets and the dresser in the bedroom, and I have to say, I couldn't afford the stuff he had on hangers and lying in drawers.

That's right. You got it. My mind started dwelling on those gambling debts. So I searched his desk for some sort of journal or financial record book. Not a damn thing in sight. However, I noticed Tolentino had a copy of *The Way by Swann's*. So the Spaniard was cultured. I couldn't resist and pulled the book off the shelf to have a brief scan, and what did I find tucked in the pages? A typed note in an envelope, no stamp, just Tolentino's name. The note said,

Mr. Tolentino,

My patience is not limitless. What you do and don't do has consequences, consequences you might find unpleasant.

If necessary, I or one of my associates will pay you a visit at your place of work.

Johnny H

After reading the note, I put it back in the book, but with the envelope just visible. I wanted the law dogs to find it when they came back with the lab boys.

The note was more than interesting. No address. No outright threat. No last name. So I'm thinking, standing there in the dead man's apartment, listening to the rain and wind pounding the

windows, *They send some gorgeous babe around, knowing Tolentino's weakness
for the ladies. He can't pay up, and she waits until Zuri leaves at 2:45 a.m., then
knocks on the door. Of course he lets her in, hoping for a second course. She tells him
it is pay up or shut up time, and he says no can do, he needs more time. She plays
it cool, letting him think time is on his side. They have a couple drinks, which she
cleans up after the deed. She lures him into the bedroom, gets him naked except for
the condom, and then whacks him. Admittedly not great, but not impossible. Except
how did she whack him? And who put the glass of wine next to* Fifty Shades? *All
I saw on the body was that small cut on his face. Poison is the obvious possibility.
Gotta get a look at the coroner's report. But even if it was poison, how the hell did
she get out of the apartment?*

10

found Piers in the bar, schmoozing the lunch crowd, which wasn't much of a crowd since it was raining like it was the end of time. I handed him the key. He asked the beautiful young thing behind the bar to pull me a pint and then took me around the bar and up to the table in the small alcove, where we would have some privacy.

"So what were you looking for?" he asked in a low tone.

"A way out," I said also keeping my voice low.

"And?"

"Nope. All the windows were locked, and there isn't even a vent someone could have climbed through to escape. Not a damn thing. However," I said, perhaps a bit too dramatically, "I did find a letter stuck in one of Silvestre's books."

"What? You said you wouldn't disturb anything."

"I didn't. The cops will never know I was there." I took a healthy drink from my pint. Piers waited impatiently. I told him about the envelope and what the note said. "What do you think? Do you know who Johnny H is?"

"Johnny H? I have no idea. I don't know what to think. It seems unlikely to me that Silvestre should be mixed up in some kind of gang trouble," he said, looking down at his hands. The rain sounded like it was going to smash the front windows.

"Listen, I didn't know the guy, but if he had a pile of gambling debts …" I let the implication hang in the air between us. "The police will find the letter. When I put it back in the book, I left it sticking out of the top. The cops are bound to see it. Count on it."

"I don't think anyone else knows about Silvestre's gambling. Or, well, what I mean is, I think he only told me, at least here at the hotel. Outside the hotel, I don't know. But I didn't tell Jacklyn or anyone else." He paused, then asked, "Have you seen Zuri Manyika? The police want to talk to her."

I shook my head but didn't say anything.

Piers continued, "Inspector Witherspoon said he would come by tomorrow morning to see her."

"Any news from the coroner?"

"No. If she's completed her report, I haven't been told."

"Did you get a chance to talk to Lily Henderson yet?" I asked.

"Yes, but she wasn't very forthcoming. She's obviously upset, but I didn't probe. It's none of my business, really. Just need her to do her job and be okay. She's a sweet kid."

We sat in silence for a moment, and then Piers stood up. "We'll see what we see. I've got to get back to work. Got to keep this place running. See you at dinner?"

"Not sure. I should get back to my day job too," I said, but in truth, I wanted to keep my options open. I was hoping to connect with Zuri, and okay, maybe get some writing done too, but my priority was Zuri. Hell, maybe Tolentino really did have a damn heart attack and I was making trouble where none should be found. But I had to admit to myself, I was troubled by the news of fighting in the apartment. And something wasn't right about Lily Henderson. I could feel it.

Piers disappeared into the guts of the hotel; I finished my pint and went to the front door. God, this hellhole rained a lot. I ran to my car, got in, but didn't drive away. I got out my cell and called Zuri. No answer. The fact that Zuri had a cell phone did not in any way compel her to answer the damn thing even if she did carry it everywhere she went. She could be that rare human being who did not have a Pavlovian response to her cell tone.

I was annoyed. I left a message asking her to call and then just sat there letting the car steam up.

In due course, I pulled myself together and drove home. The rain continued to fall heavy on this small, indifferent, Victorian museum of a town. There really was nothing else to do but wait, so I was determined to put in a full day with my space cowboy and his blue lover. I made myself a sandwich, got a glass of carbonated water, and set up in the front room. I put the fire on low, placed the small table from my study next to the chair in the bay window for my lunch, sat down with my laptop on my knees, settled in, and listened to the rain on the windows. Nothing more to do. No Zuri. No coroner's report. No way out of the apartment other than walking through the door. And no movement on gambling debts from the doughnut patrol.

Let's face it. It didn't take much to convince the mysterious, but not unapproachable, Rashida to hitch a ride on the *Liberté C57-D* to wherever the ship and crew were going. Chad Steel, always man enough to be a gentleman, gave her her own sleeping quarters, though not far from his own. The *Liberté C57-D* lifted off from what Chad Steel mockingly called Planet Wetworld in the Crux-Scutum inner galactic arm and headed for Omicron^2 Centauri, an A-type supergiant of a sun in the constellation of Centaurus. The news had come to Chad Steel on Planet Wetworld that a high level assassination had occurred in the Omicron^2 Centauri System, which meant the entire lucrative trading franchise of all the o^2 Gen worlds was up for grabs. To say "trading franchise" was, of course, partly true and partly misleading. Yes, there was big money to be made in legit trading within the o^2 Gen System and, through its business, with the rest of the galaxy. But there was also a more nefarious side to o^2 Gen finance, and everyone knew it. If you were looking to feed your gambling habits, o^2 Gen was the place to go, and word was that the assassination was somehow linked to some galaxy-size gambling debts. In any case, Chad Steel aimed to be in the mix.

There was another reason Chad Steel was heading for the o^2 Gen System at warp speed. On Planet Wetworld he had been warned by an old colleague and friend that the blue princess he was bedding was somehow implicated in the assassination! Chad Steel had questions swirling around in that brilliant mind of his, and he aimed to find the answers. Did his apparently innocent meeting with Rashida happen by chance, or did she arrange it? Was this something between them real or a setup? He could usually read people like a book, but Rashida … He was willing to take a chance on her, but also, being the man he was, he could dump her at a moment's notice if things didn't add up to his liking. And finally, was Rashida a murderer? Perhaps a high-caliber assassin for hire? Chad Steel was sure he would find the answers in the o^2 Gen System, or he would die trying.

11

Just as the *Liberté C57-D* was about to enter the o² Gen System, my doorbell rang. I assumed it was Kelly or Parker asking if I wanted to come over for dinner, but when I got downstairs and opened the front door, there was Zuri dripping wet with a plastic bag of groceries hanging from each hand. "I hear you've been trying to get in touch," she said and smiled.

I was so stunned I just stood there. Her rental car, much nicer than my shitmobile, was parked out front. She'd still gotten soaked running from the car to the door.

"Well, can I come in? I've got dinner for us, just like in the movies," she said.

I let her in, of course. We took the groceries to the kitchen, but before unpacking and preparing dinner, she told me that the meeting with the cops was set up for late morning the next day at the hotel.

"I assume you knew the police wanted to talk to me again," she said.

"Yes, I did. I've been trying to reach you to give you a heads-up," I said. "So … a fight."

"Oh God, you heard about that?" she said, not a little anxious.

"More to the point, the fuzz have heard about it. Why else did you think they wanted to talk to you again?"

"Well, I was hoping just some kind of follow-up. Okay, thanks for letting me know," she said. She stood looking at the floor, the groceries, then said, "Right. Let's make a deal. For tonight, let's not talk about it. Let's talk about anything but the police and poor Silvestre. Okay?"

"Deal," I said, thinking the last thing I wanted to talk about was Tolentino!

I'm not the kind to kiss and tell—well, actually, I am the kind to kiss and tell, I'm a fucking reporter on the *Fremont Argus News* for heaven's sake. If you don't write kiss and tell stories in Fremont, you spend a lot of time just sitting on your ass. So let me rephrase that. I don't kiss and tell about *my* life. Still, I think it's permissible to say that it was a great night. Not only is Zuri the best lover I've ever had, and I've had more than a baker's dozen, she can cook!

Being quite handy in the kitchen myself—no hamburger-meat Drake—I put on my apron, which impressed her. We cut and diced and sautéed while drinking a good red I had been saving for a better day. This was that day in spades. We put the food, plates, and silverware on two trays and carried them upstairs. I put some music on, cranked up the fire, and closed the curtains in the bay window to shut out the weather as Zuri set the table. We ate. We drank. We talked. We flirted. And when we went to the back bedroom, we redefined the oft-used and abused phrase "to make love." If truth be told, I learned more about Zuri's delicious body and abundant desires in two hours than I had about Kaitlyn Lethbridge's in two years. I slept well that night, let me tell you.

The next morning the sun was shining full-on, and there was not even a whisper of wind. We awoke early, showered together, and got dressed. I made java and toast, and we sat in the front room, enjoying the warmth of the sun and our memories from the previous night. Damn good memories, and I was hoping to make a whole scrapbook full of them.

Zuri left in plenty of time to get back to the hotel, change, and compose herself for the interview with Inspector Witherspoon. I had another cup of joe and decided to walk to the Skinburness. It is downright stupid not to take advantage of the sun when it reluctantly agrees to show its face. And a walk along the promenade when the wind wasn't trying to throw me into the Solway was a rare opportunity.

It had been arranged to meet once again in Piers's office. When I got there, Piers and Zuri were sitting quietly, with a large coffeepot and cups on the table in front of them. I took a seat next to Zuri and smiled at her. Piers gave me a quizzical look.

Before I could pour myself a cup, both Witherspoon and Jamison arrived. As before, PC Jamison would hardly say a word but would take copious notes.

Inspector Witherspoon sat across from Zuri and began the proceedings. "Ms. Manyika, I hope you realize that we are doing you a courtesy by coming out here to the hotel to continue our interview with you," he said.

"Yes, of course, and I'm very grateful. But why don't we get right to it? I understand that the argument I had with Mr. Tolentino was overheard," Zuri said. She seemed composed and self-assured, but I couldn't tell if it was only a front.

"Hmm, that's right," Inspector Witherspoon said with some hesitation, taken slightly by surprise. "Someone has filled you in?"

"Well, Drake did mention it last night," she said, looking over to me. Inspector Witherspoon looked my way as well, more than a little annoyed.

"I don't see the harm, Inspector," I said in my defense. "Ms. Manyika has a right to know."

"Yes, certainly, but I would have preferred to have conducted the interview in my own way. You are a guest here, Mr. Ramsey. I suggest you don't forget it," Witherspoon said. "Ms. Manyika, I don't know how much Mr. Ramsey told you—"

"Not much," I interrupted. I didn't know much, just that one of the folks staying at the hotel heard a fight. I found it interesting that, since Piers was the only person who could have given me the information, Witherspoon didn't draw him into this little tug-of-war. I certainly wasn't going to. Piers just sat there cool as cool could be.

Witherspoon ignored me and continued addressing Zuri. "A customer here in the hotel couldn't sleep and was apparently wandering around the hotel, looking for the library. He came down to the ground floor and heard a loud argument coming from down the hall, the hall that leads to Mr. Tolentino's flat. This at 2:45 a.m., to be precise. Is there anything you want to add to the statement you made a couple of days ago?"

Zuri was silent for a moment but never broke eye contact with Witherspoon.

"Ms. Zuri," PC Jamison said rather sharply, "we can do this downtown if you like."

I looked at Jamison and smiled to myself, thinking, *That's rich. Downtown! Where the hell is downtown? Wigton doesn't have a fucking downtown. Damn drama queen.*

"No, that won't be necessary," Zuri said, without even glancing Jamison's way. All her attention was focused on Inspector Witherspoon. "Can I assume you want the gory details, Inspector?"

"I think that goes without saying," he said.

"Okay. I went to Mr. Tolentino's apartment at about one o'clock, when he had finished his duties. I sat on the sofa, and he went to the kitchen to get a bottle of wine and glasses. We sat on the sofa for, I guess, half an hour, drinking the wine and talking, though as we talked, Mr. Tolentino would touch my arm occasionally. Somewhere in the middle of my telling him about my work in New Orleans, Mr. Tolentino slid over toward me and began kissing me. I've been with worse." Zuri paused and took a sip of coffee and then continued.

"Before long we were naked and having sex on the sofa. I have to say, Mr. Tolentino was quite the little expert. We finished our lovemaking, oh, I guess shortly after two o'clock. I asked for a blanket to wrap up in, and Mr. Tolentino went to what I presume was his bedroom and came back with a small blanket."

Confession. That bit about Tolentino being "quite a little expert" did not sit well with me. I wondered if Zuri had compared me to that little toad last night.

"You never entered the bedroom?" Inspector Witherspoon asked.

"No. As I said, we had sex on the sofa in the living room. It was plenty big enough, and I sensed that Mr. Tolentino enjoyed having sex there. I guess it added a bit more excitement for the dear man."

"So you wrapped up in the blanket. And Mr. Tolentino, did he get dressed?"

"No. We both remained naked, but I wanted to cover myself. After all, I didn't really know Mr. Tolentino that well, and I didn't feel totally comfortable with him staring at me."

"You both remained naked? Why didn't you get dressed when you were done?" asked Witherspoon.

"Inspector, people often remain naked after having sex. Surely people in Wigton have been known to sit around naked in their own homes," Zuri said.

I sensed that she was trying to embarrass Inspector Witherspoon, and it was working. She might have been born in Zimbabwe, but she was an American girl now. She'd take no prisoners. I realized she was becoming more uncomfortable as she spoke; perhaps she wanted to deflect some of that onto her interrogator.

"I'm just trying to ascertain the details of the situation, Ms. Manyika. Please continue."

"Well, I sat curled up in the blanket, hugging my knees. Mr. Tolentino removed his condom in the bathroom, as I said before, came back still naked, and sat down next to me. He put one arm across the back of the sofa and the other on my knee. We drank the rest of the wine, and he went to the kitchen to get a second bottle. He came back to the sofa, opened the bottle, filled our glasses, and then sat down very close to me. It was two forty-five. He began kissing me and, with his hands, pushed my legs down. He then began caressing my breasts and kissing me harder. I was not pleased and not inclined to have a second go with him. He was a nice man, but his tone had changed. He was becoming aggressive.

"His hand slid down between my legs, and he tried to touch my anus. I pulled away. He pinned my shoulders back against the sofa and said he wanted to have anal sex. He pulled off the blanket and quickly, forcibly turned my body, trying to make me lie on my stomach. I swung back and slapped him. I think my ring cut his face. I got up, grabbed my clothes, and left the apartment. I walked around the corner in the hallway, quickly got dressed, and then went to my room. I showered. What had begun as a fun evening with a charming man ended as a nightmare. I was shaking. Once I felt clean, I went to bed. It was three fifteen.

"That's it, Inspector, and I hope PC Jamison there got it all down. I don't want to repeat it." She put down the cup she had been holding throughout. She was shaking. She took a deep breath, composed herself, and sat back in her chair.

The room was silent for what seemed like a long time. After all, we were four men with one woman. Attempted anal rape sat on the table in front of us all. Piers was openly disturbed. He started to say something to Zuri and then thought better of it. The sun shone brightly in the window, offering no shadows in which to hide. Zuri, now that she had completed her accounting of the night with Tolentino, seemed to have regained her composure. She certainly was a strong woman. I got the sense that she had been around the block more than a few times herself, and that they were damn big, dirty blocks.

Inspector Witherspoon seemed to be at a loss as to how to continue, or rather bring the interview to an end. Jamison didn't even pretend to know. Witherspoon finally thanked Zuri for her detailed account, which he acknowledged must have been difficult for her, and then said, "Ms. Manyika, I'm afraid I will need to take your ring as evidence. It will be returned to you in due course."

"I thought you might want it, so I brought it along," Zuri said, reaching into her jacket pocket. PC Jamison quickly took an evidence bag from his uniform pocket, and Zuri dropped the ring into the bag.

As both Wigton cops got up to leave, Piers asked if the coroner's report was available.

"Not yet," said Witherspoon. "The coroner's got her hands full right now. I'll let you know when it's available."

Hands full! I thought. *Doing what? Autopsying cows?* I was itching to know how the Spaniard had died.

"If you like, you can come to the station when I've got it, " he said as he was leaving. Piers agreed. I knew he would let me tag along.

Since it was such a beautiful day, Zuri and I decided to drive down to the Lake District and find a country pub for lunch. Her car. Piers gave us direction to the Hare and Hounds, a sixteenth-century pub and inn in the village of Levens near Kendal. As she sped around the curves, proving what the car could do, Zuri's mood lifted with each passing mile.

I, on the other hand, was filled with thoughts and anxieties. A second scenario for Silvestre Tolentino's death kept running around in my mind, demanding attention like one of those little screaming brats in restaurants whose parents can't control him. Unfortunately, it was a more plausible scenario then the one I had concocted about a female mobster killing the Spaniard. I kept thinking, *Zuri doesn't wear jewelry. I've never seen her wear rings, earrings, necklaces. Nothing. So she has a ring coated with some poison and strikes Tolentino across the face, thus poisoning him. The poison takes effect after she leaves, and voilà, the locked-room mystery is solved. One thing though. The condom on his penis? Simple. He puts it on before the fight, thinking he's going to have a second round with Zuri. She simply leaves that out of her story. The fight? Well, Zuri cooks up a reason for a fight so she can smack him a hard one. Or maybe she just belts him out of the blue.*

But why would she want to kill Tolentino?

12

When I awoke the next morning, Zuri was lying beside me. It was hard not to take her seriously. I rolled over and spooned her, with the expected results. Just as we finished doing what the morning demanded, my cell rang. I sat on the edge of the bed in the cold and groped for my phone. It was Kelly. She had completed her initial research into the deaths at the hotel and was asking me over for coffee and conversation. I said yes, of course, and indicated that someone would be accompanying me.

I introduced Kelly and Zuri. Kelly was aware that by all accounts Zuri was the last person to see Silvestre Tolentino alive, but she didn't say anything. Don't get me wrong. Kelly could kill with a look alone, but she was also quick to accept and slow to judge. And she was curious.

As we went into the kitchen, where Kelly had hot water dripping on coffee beans, and scrambled eggs and toast on the ready, I was eager to hear what she had to say about the hotel deaths. But for some reason she wanted to make small talk, and she kept staring at Zuri. It started to make me impatient and even uncomfortable. It finally came out, Kelly being Kelly.

"I heard you are from Zimbabwe, Zuri," Kelly said over her coffee. "You sure don't sound like you're from Zimbabwe. I'd say you were American through and through."

How Kelly had got ahold of the Zimbabwe link, God only knows. But she seemed to know everything about everybody around here.

Zuri laughed and said, "Well, I sure worked on it, so thanks. I was born and raised in Highfield, a suburb of Harare, but my mother sent me to live with her sister and her husband in New York when I was eight."

"God, you must have missed her. Eight is young to leave your mother," Kelly said.

"I did. It broke my heart, and I missed my friends terribly. We said we'd keep in touch, but of course we didn't. The only people I really kept in touch with over time, besides my mom and brother, were my cousins Chantall and Nelson. Chantall and I were like sisters. We both lived in Highfield, went to the same church and school. We spent a lot of time running around the sandy streets of Highfield in our bare feet. When I first arrived in New York I used to cry myself to sleep. But I never cried when my aunt and uncle could see!

"I understood why my mother sent me to New York. She did it for my future. Even as children, we used to talk about getting out of Zimbabwe and going to South Africa or England or America. I remember once some church people visiting from England on a church exchange program. One of them asked my mother if she would leave Zimbabwe if she had the chance. My mother said, and I remember this clearly, 'If you have children and you have the chance to leave, it would be irresponsible not to.' So, when my aunt said she would take me, well, that was that. It was difficult, but I understood what my mother was doing. Nelson eventually left too. He's in London. He's English now, just like I'm American."

"You're a US citizen?" Kelly asked.

"Yes. In order to survive, I had to become American as fast as I could. The kids either avoided me or teased me unmercifully. So I taught myself to sound like an American girl and act like an American girl. I worked hard, made friends, did well in school. So, yeah, I guess I am American now. But I still go home at least once a year, mostly to visit my mother and my cousin, but also to remind myself that I'm African."

As fascinating as all this was, I wanted to move on and get the dirt on the Skinburness. So I jumped in and explained to Zuri what was up. She was as surprised as I had been to hear there had been twelve deaths in the Skinburness Hotel since its opening. Kelly had printed out her report but summarized her findings as we ate eggs and drank java. Here's the lowdown.

She had found fairly good details on all the murder victims except two, not surprisingly the first and the second. Still, all the victims had the following things in common:

- All were male.
- All died in the Edwin Hodge Banks West Wing.
- All were found in the nude.
- All were declared dead by natural causes.

Other data varied:

- Their ages ranged from twenty-five to sixty-seven years old.

- Four victims were from England, two from Scotland, two from the United States, one from Wales, and one from Spain (Silvestre Tolentino).

- Seven of the deaths occurred in room 217, four in various other rooms in the west wing, and one (again Silvestre Tolentino) in the hotel staff quarters.

- Ten had no obvious physical marks on their bodies, and there were no signs of violence; there was no report on two of the victims.

- Eight were married and four single.

- Six were associated with rumors and legends speculating that they were victims of a ghostly apparition in the hotel.

I asked Kelly to e-mail copies to Piers and me. I very much hoped that last bit about murderous ghosts didn't find its way to Kara and Libbie. I'd never hear the end of it. But I might have known that Kelly and Zuri would pick up on it.

"I was intrigued by the rumors and legends surrounding the deaths, and by the fact that seven of them happened in room 217," Kelly said.

"Oh, please, Kelly. Not you," I said, feeling a bad case of frustration coming on.

"Drake, there have been rumors for years, forever, that the Skinburness Hotel is haunted."

"I don't believe in ghosts, and ghosts don't kill people," I said, a little exasperated.

"Perhaps," Zuri joined in, to my dismay. "But a *belief* in ghosts can kill. Surely you're not so closed-minded as to deny that possibility."

I remained silent, hoping this would all go away. It didn't.

"I believe that," Kelly said.

"I did some work on it from a cross-cultural perspective," Zuri said.

"What do you mean, 'did some work'? What are you talking about?" I asked.

"You've never asked what I do to stay alive," Zuri said.

"No, I guess not. I've been preoccupied," I said to the sound of Kelly's laughter.

"I bet," Kelly said.

"I work as a professor and researcher in African, African American, and cross-cultural studies at Loyola University in New Orleans," she said.

"Where'd you get your degree?" Kelly asked.

"Stanford University."

Okay, I was impressed. I said, "So do I have to call you Dr. Manyika now?"

"If you want," Zuri said.

"And I guess you know something about ghost beliefs and murder?"

"I didn't say anything about murder. But do you really want to know? I don't want to waste my time."

"Waste your time! That's what time is for in Silloth," I countered.

"I want to know. Forget him. Tell me," Kelly said, pouring another cup of joe for everyone.

"Well …" Zuri began. She was enjoying this at my expense, at least a little. "People die for the strangest of reasons. There are many names for it. Anthropologists and others refer to 'bone-pointing syndrome' and 'voodoo death.' Both are also known by the names 'psychogenic death' or 'psychosomatic death.' Among the Arrernte people of Australia, the *kurdaitcha*, or the *illapurinja*, the female *kurdaitcha*, can kill literally by pointing a bone at a person. The same is true of the *quesalid*, a Kwakiutl shaman in the Pacific

Northwest. A man by the name of Walter Cannon wrote that if a person who broke some societal taboo was accused by a *kurdaitcha* or shaman or witch doctor in the bone-pointing ceremony, that person would *expect* to die. The ceremony and the beliefs held by the person and the community can be seen as the cause of death. The fear can be overwhelming, to the point where the person's health deteriorates due to the psychological distress. A person can die within twenty-four hours after the initial accusation and ceremony. The pointing of the bone, or the equivalent in differing societies, is a curse of death.

"Claude Lévi-Strauss wrote about this. He used examples from witchcraft among the Zuni in the American Southwest and the Nambicuara shaman in the Amazonian rain forest, as well as the Australian and Pacific examples. Lévi-Strauss said three things come into play: the shaman, the victim, and the community, all of whom participate in the ceremony. The shaman believes in his power to affect a person's physical condition by calling upon whatever supernatural spirits or guides he is in relationship with. The victim believes in the shaman's power and that he or she is vulnerable to the spirits called upon. Finally, the beliefs and expectations of the shaman and the victim are reinforced by the public's participation and belief in the realities that structure their existence. The victim believes he or she will die, and the community treats them as if they are dead, for die they must.

"Don't get hung up on spirit worlds and not believing in curses. There have been many recorded incidents where people died under these circumstances. What happens is very physiological and explainable. Fear causes a rush of adrenaline, an overdose of adrenaline, which can affect a lot of our organs, but most importantly the heart. Fear takes over and kills. And not just in what you in the West call 'native societies.' Similar deaths have been recorded in concentration camps and prisoner of war camps. It happens. If someone believes a ghost is out to get them, they could die."

When Zuri had finished what I took as a minilecture, we all sat in silence, drinking our coffee and killing off the eggs. Me? Well, I was ... Okay, to be honest, a little intimidated. Who the hell was this African princess anyway? And what was she doing playing with me? Well, yes. Playing! Was that all she was doing?

Kelly broke the silence. "You should have a look at room 217."

"Why? You think I'm going to find some bones?" I asked.

"Now Drake, sweetie," Zuri said, "let's not get all snooty. There is more in this universe than your Fremont, California, worldview."

"You both want me to go looking for a ghost?"

"Wait, wait, wait," Kelly said. "There's something else. Well, actually, two something elses. First, you know the old vicar who comes by almost every day, thinking he lives here?"

"Yeah, of course. The old boy gives me the creeps," I said. Then, turning to Zuri, "The old vicar of the C of E church wanders around Silloth. This house used to be his vicarage, and he keeps coming back, thinking he still lives here. It's worse than *The Twilight Zone*."

"I think I've seen him. Dresses in black and walks sort of bent over and really slowly?" Zuri asked.

"That's the guy. What about him?" I asked, looking at Kelly.

"Well, something he said clicked with some of the research I did. The ghost stories associated with the Skinburness Hotel hint at a woman of light, or something like that. And I remember the old vicar saying over and over again, 'She's so light.'"

I remembered him stopping me on the sidewalk that time. I thought he said, "She's so white." I looked at Kelly and said, "That doesn't make sense, 'She's so light.'"

"I know, but the stories ... And there is another thing. I started checking into the vicar's history, talking to some of the older members of the church. This will amaze you. When he retired, he moved into a bungalow up the road on the way to Skinburness. His wife, kids, and some people from the church threw him a surprise party at the Skinburness Hotel. It was a big deal for back then. Dinner in the restaurant and a room for the night. Anyway, the story goes that his wife couldn't sleep. So she went to the library, and when she returned to the room, she saw a flash of light and the dear old man lying on the bed, completely naked, staring at the ceiling. They say he has never been the same since. And get this. He was in room 217!"

Okay. I admit that was a bit creepy, "creepy" being the word that always comes to mind when I see the old guy.

"Well, what do you think?" asked Kelly, with more than a little challenge in her voice.

"I think you should tell me what the second something else is," I said.

"Jacklyn told me that the ghost was somehow associated with a statue in the hotel. A white marble statue of a woman. And sure enough, there is such a statue in the hallway leading to the Edwin Hodge Banks Wing. I went over and took a couple of pictures." As she pulled the photos from a green folder lying on the table, she asked Zuri, "Have you seen it?"

"No. I'm in the east wing and haven't really wandered around the hotel that much, except for the exercise room, library ... You know, the public places," Zuri said.

"Well, I did some checking, and here's what I found," Kelly said. "The building was designed in 1878 by an architect named Charles John Ferguson. Edwin Hodge Banks built it in the 1880s for £22,000. I can't find the date the construction was completed, but I have a guess. Banks lived in Wigton and owned a small cotton mill. They refer to him as a wealthy country gentleman, maybe because he had a thirty-foot steam yacht he called the *Neptune* moored in the Solway. He went bankrupt in 1889 and, as far as I can see, disappeared from the area. Banks's property was transferred to George F. Brown, who took over ownership of the hotel in 1889.

"I looked at early photos of the hotel, and I think the statue has been sitting in the same place since the hotel opened. According to some documentation Jacklyn showed me, in 1885 a man by the name of Montgomery Fielding gave the statue to the Skinburness. I think the hotel was actually completed in 1885 and the statue has been in the passageway since the opening. The Fielding family lived, lives, in Hampstead in northwest London. Montgomery Fielding's granddaughter, Sybil Fielding, is still alive and is living in the Hampstead family home. She never married so was easy to find.

"So we've got twelve deaths, the vicar, the woman of light, the statue, room 217, and dear old Sybil Fielding in Hampstead." Kelly sat back rather satisfied.

"Somebody shoot me and put me out of my misery," I said.

13

The Wigton coppers were on the way to the Skinburness when Piers called me. Zuri and I had said our good-byes at Kelly's door in the late morning, and I went to my place to both digest and exorcise what Kelly had reported. Piers's phone call was a welcome splash of reality. The cops were on their way to his office to question him about Tolentino's gambling debt. Sure as shit, they had found the letter tucked away in the book. They had also identified the mysterious Johnny H, the writer of the letter. I snapped out of my altered state and hightailed it to the hotel.

When I got to the hotel, Piers was already with the good inspector and his loyal PC, so I went to the Cullingworths' apartment and bummed a cup of joe from the girls. Jacklyn was in the kitchen preparing puds. Basil was supervising. From the kitchen window I saw the cops getting in their car and driving out of the parking lot.

I took my coffee and went to Piers's office. He was more than eager to fill me in.

This was the dirty on Silvestre Tolentino and Johnny H, according to Inspector Witherspoon and the ever-silent PC Bill Jamison. John Humphreys, a.k.a. Johnny H, was the proud owner of Casanova Menswear on Cuthbert's Lane in Carlisle. The Casanova was an upmarket men's clothing store, from the sounds of it too upmarket for me, though not for Tolentino. Dear Granny sure wouldn't have approved of me spending her dosh on fancy, expensive clothes. Carlisle's law dogs had long suspected that the Casanova was really a front for other, let's say, questionable activities, but no amount of digging could find anything untoward. Looked like Johnny H was just a legit businessman helping Carlisle men look like they lived in London or Paris.

So why the flatfoot suspicions? I asked myself, sitting in Piers's office. There was the tenuous link that Johnny H liked playing the horses, but hell, so does the freakin' Queen of England.

As it turned out, Tolentino had gotten to know Johnny H during his frequent visits to the Casanova. Tolentino liked the ladies and liked looking the part. The right clothes were a must. He and Johnny H would go to the track together, and when he started tumbling into debt, Johnny H agreed to help him out. All on the up-and-up, I should add. Johnny H got his lawyer to do the right and proper, and Tolentino scribbled his John Hancock on the dotted line.

When the Carlisle fuzz, with Inspector Witherspoon in attendance, pressed Johnny H on the note found in Tolentino's book, he just laughed. It was a joke between friends. Tolentino had started paying back the loan, insisted Johnny H. The paperwork backed him up, but at the rate of payment it was clear that both Johnny H and Tolentino would be well underground before the debt was wiped. And on top of that, Tolentino didn't stop playing the ponies just because he was in hock to Mr. Casanova. So, when push came to shove, Johnny H's comeback to the cops' questions was as old as dark alleys and gambling chumps. Why would he want to harm Tolentino when the man still owed him money?

No matter how you sliced it, facts were facts. There was no evidence that Tolentino owed anyone else money from his gambling debts. The legal agreement between Tolentino and Johnny H was sound, and Johnny H had been in New York the night Tolentino died, buying some fancy line or other of men's clothing for the Casanova and the overly sanguine men of Cumbria.

"You know, Piers," I said, "maybe Johnny H hired someone to do his dirty work for him and put the heat on Silvestre. Maybe some femme fatale, since it was known by most of the sentient universe that Silvestre liked the ladies."

"We're back to the same old problem," Piers said. "How did this femme fatale, as you put it, get out of the flat?"

"Poison," I said.

"Perhaps," Piers said, turning to look at the window. He knew I was stretching, and he knew why. If Johnny H was the killer, then Zuri wasn't. He turned back to me. "But it's just speculation until we hear the coroner's report."

Piers was right, of course. The Spaniard had been dead for four days, and we were still waiting on that damn autopsy. You'd think they had a shitload of murders happening every day.

The poison angle was paradoxical. It would explain the locked-room mystery, but it pointed the finger at Zuri as much as Johnny H. Actually, more. The Johnny H scenario necessitated the introduction of a second actor, a person hired to polish off the vic. The case against Zuri needed no such accomplice. Okay, she had explained the fight she had with Tolentino, but she had been nervous and it hadn't played well. Not to mention that attempted rape wasn't a bad motive for murder. She had more work to do if she wanted to escape police scrutiny.

And then Zuri Manyika disappeared.

14

had been calling Zuri for three days with no luck when Kelly asked me to meet her at a café in Wigton. She had taken her car in for servicing and wanted a lift back to Silloth. But first she wanted to talk, privately, and a small café in Wigton on a cold, wet morning was pretty damn private.

Wigton is an old market town that still has an actual market and a cattle auction. Kelly and Parker took me to the auction one day so I could "experience the real Cumbria." Yeah, right. I guess it's a nice enough town except when the wind blows south and the stench from Innovia Films, called the Factory by the natives, settles in each and every crevice. The Factory is best known for making cellophane and Propafilm, and to make that stuff you gotta also make a real stench. No one bitches, however, because it employs most people in town.

We met at a dump of a café on the narrow main street of

Wigton. It was still pretty early, and the café was chilly, damp, and empty except for the woman sweeping the floor. I thought for a moment it was closed. There were no opening times posted so it was hard to tell. But then I saw Kelly sitting at a table by the front window. When I sat down across from her, she gave me a look that said something serious was on her mind.

The woman stopped sweeping and slowly made her way over to our table. Kelly ordered tea. I ordered coffee saying, "Cup of coffee, black, and it would be nice if it had been brewed this year." Kelly shot me a dirty look, and the waitress cum cleaner simply turned and walked away. My hero Philip Marlowe said that, or something like that, in *The Big Sleep*, and I had always wanted to try it out. Though my delivery might have lacked PI nonchalance, it seemed an appropriate time and place to go for it. The woman brought me a lukewarm instant coffee with milk, just made. I guess I deserved that.

"Listen. I've got some news about your girlfriend you need to hear," Kelly began.

"What the hell do you mean?"

"Well, I had some time, so I looked into Zuri Manyika and came up with some pretty disturbing information. We really need to talk."

"I didn't tell you to look into Zuri. I told you ..."

"I know! But you'll be glad I did," she interrupted.

I doubted it. I was a bit unnerved. I'd been waiting around for three days. I knew Zuri had had a fight with Tolentino and smacked him across the face. If she had poisoned him with her ring, then okay, our locked-room mystery was solved. But let's face it: that was not the way I wanted things to end. The cops were playing shadow to her every move. And then, bam, she up and disappeared. I didn't know how much more bad news I could take. Zuri as a femme fatale? Perhaps, but at least she should be *my* femme fatale.

"Do we have to do this now?" I asked, sitting in that freezing cold excuse of a café.

"Drake, you've got to hear this. And not with your dick."

I thought that was a little unkind, but said nothing.

"Your Zuri killed a man in Harare. She may be wanted for murder," she said and then sat back to enjoy the impact.

Now that was news! Nonetheless, I played it cool.

"What the hell are you talking about?" I said. Cool, just stay cool.

"On the Internet. It was in the *Herald*, a Harare paper. It said some men entered her house one night and she shot one of them dead. They were Zanu-PF men. They were there on official business, and they said that the killing was politically motivated. Zuri wasn't held. There wasn't a lot to it, just that she shot a man in her mother's home in Highfield, that suburb of Harare where Zuri said she was raised as a little girl. I looked and looked to see if the police in Harare were pursuing her or had got in touch with the police in New Orleans, but I couldn't find anything. I assume they're looking for her."

"Is that it?"

"That's all I could find. But the point is, if the police here know about this, then Zuri's got to be a prime suspect in Silvestre Tolentino's death."

Kelly was right. What a fucking morning. I looked out the window and a low, dark grayness hung over Wigton like a weight.

"What is that?" I asked Kelly, not looking at her.

"What? What is what?" Kelly said.

"That! That thing in the middle of the intersection?"

"Why?"

"I'm just curious."

"Drake, Zuri killed a man. The police will arrest her if they find out."

"Kelly, what the hell is it?" I asked, looking back at her.

"Oh, God. It's the George Moore Memorial Fountain. He built it in the late 1800s for his wife who died. You see that square bronze relief? There is one on each side of the memorial, all likenesses of his wife. He called them the Acts of Mercy."

I finished my cold instant brown coffee and Kelly finished her cold brown tea and we left. Neither of us said a word on the twelve miles or so to Silloth. I parked my shitmobile. I went to my front door and she to hers. But before she entered, she said, "Drake, I'm sorry. What do you want me to do next?"

I looked at her. We were both getting wet, so I just shook my head and said, "I'm not sure. Why don't we talk about it later today? Kelly, do you think she murdered a man?"

"Actually, no, I don't think she murdered anyone. But she did apparently kill someone and—"

"I know. Big cop and little cop will be all over her if they find out," I said.

15

When I closed the door, I just stood in the entrance for a moment to collect my thoughts. I looked down the long, narrow, gloomy hallway to the kitchen and then up the stairs to my living quarters. Despite the utterly horrible dark-patterned wallpaper and the filthy carpet, I started to feel a little better. If Kelly said Zuri was no murderer, that was good enough for me. Kelly could read people like a cheap paperback novel.

I went upstairs, sat in the front room by the bay window, and tried calling Zuri. No answer. Of course I left a message, as I had been doing for three days. I hadn't been over to the Skinburness Hotel, my excuse being that I had to get back to my day job. In fact, if I was honest with myself, I was avoiding the hotel because I knew I would go straight to the corridor connecting the east and west wings, looking for that damn statue. And I'd probably ask to see room 217 too!

I decided it was best to turn off thoughts about Zuri, Johnny H, room 217, statues, the whole damn lot. I got my laptop and turned my attention to Chad Steel.

I docked the *Liberté C57-D* in orbit around the capital planet Betelgeuse of the Omicron² Centauri System. Betelgeuse was named after the giant red star in the Orion Constellation for reasons that have been lost to history. As the capital planet in the o² Gen System it was the place to be and, therefore, a frequent destination for Chad Steel.

It was dark when Chad Steel, Rashida, and the crew shuttled down to Betelgeuse. Rashida disappeared into the night for a prearranged meeting with an unknown companion. Little did Chad Steel know, she would disappear for days.

Being known throughout the galaxy and having been several times to Betelgeuse, Chad Steel had no problem getting the lowdown on current events. The presumed assassination of the o² Gen System leader, known simply as S. T., was a mystery. He was found dead in his mansion, which possessed the most sophisticated and reliable security system known in the galaxy. How a killer got in and out without detection was a complete and utter mystery to the authorities. Put simply, it was impossible. Thus the story circulated that S. T. had been killed by a representative of the all-but-omnipotent Agnians, an ancient species evolved from mortals from another galaxy. Legend has it that the Agnians could suck the life out of any human being whose misfortune it was to encounter them. To Chad Steel, who had been around the galaxy more than a few times and had faced the worst of what it had to offer, such legends were stories to frighten children. Chad Steel did not frighten. Steel by name, steel by nature.

What was more disturbing to Chad Steel was the information he gathered in a dark and dirty bar on the edge of the city. While the authorities dismissed the rumors that Rashida was involved in the murder of S. T., it was well known that she had killed with both pistol and knife. Who was this sky-blue vixen, perhaps the only woman in the galaxy who could demand Chad Steel's heart? As Chad Steel was leaving the dirty bar in the dead of night, heavy with thoughts of murder and love, it started to rain.

And my cell phone rang.

My cell told me, unemotionally, that it was Zuri. I almost hesitated to answer. It was night. Where the hell had she been for three days? And why had she ignored me? I tucked my anger away for safekeeping and tapped the green Accept button.

When I inquired where she had been, she ignored my question and instead asked me to meet her at the docks near the entrance to the mill. I looked at the clock. It was 10:34 p.m. The prospect of going out wasn't inviting. It was raining and blowing like the wind gods were pissed. But she sounded nervous, or maybe frightened, so of course I stepped up. That's just who I am. I mean, if it's two outs in the bottom of the ninth with the bases loaded, and you're down by three, you put me in. No-brainer. I told her I'd meet her, wondering what the hell she was doing out at the mill at night in this weather.

Silloth actually has a pretty busy port, shipping wheat, fertilizer, molasses, and such. Carrs Flour Mill was built during the late 1800s next to what was then called the New Dock. It's now the biggest player in town, which isn't saying much.

When I opened my front door, I instantly realized that an umbrella was useless and dropped it in the entrance. I pulled my collar up and headed out. I bent my body into the wind and rain and ran to my car, thinking, *If I don't get out of here, I'll metamorphose into a fucking Sillothean.* Within seconds I was drenched.

As I approached the docks, I saw Zuri sheltering from the elements in a small, open, shedlike structure. There was a lone lightbulb with a metal shade hanging from a pole. The bulb's dim light formed a cone in the darkness that lit one corner of the shed. Zuri was standing at the edge of darkness and light, her trench coat tied tight around her waist and buttoned up to her chin. The collar partially hid her face. She had an old-fashioned bell hat pulled down over her forehead. Her hands were stuffed in her pockets, but when I stepped into the shed's entrance, she threw her arms around me and held me tight. She was trembling, but I couldn't tell if it was because of the cold and wet or because she was scared. I suspected both.

"Where the hell have you been? I've been trying to call you for three days. And what the hell are you doing out here?" I said close to her ear as she still held me.

"I went to my cousin Nelson's. I think I'm in trouble. I should have known. How could he be one of them? What am I going to do? I shouldn't have come back here. I should have gone someplace else."

"Slow down. You aren't making any sense. You've just gone all the way to London for three lousy days? What for? Why didn't you tell me?"

"It's Nelson. He called me. He said Chantall was coming from Highfield. I was in my car practically before I hung up the phone."

"You drove? Why the hell did you drive? That's three hundred miles—more than three hundred. Why didn't you take the train?"

"Chantall's like my sister. I couldn't wait to see her. Oh, Drake, I'm so scared!"

"So, what, you and Chantall had a fight or something?"

"A fight? No, of course not. She was wonderful. Everything was wonderful. She said my mom was doing okay. I was so happy with them; we had such a good time. We sat up late eating peanut butter sandwiches like when we were kids. But last night in bed I started to wonder. Why did she come? What is she doing here? Nobody's got any money. It's Nelson and I who send money to them, and God knows we haven't got a lot. There's no way she could have afforded that plane ticket, no matter how much she wanted to see me. No way. I lay there for hours trying to think of any other explanation. But there isn't one. Somebody had to pay for that ticket. She's leading them to me. She and Nelson. There's no other explanation. If I'd stayed another day, it might have been too late.

"I've got to hide. Drake, I'm so, so sorry. I didn't want to get you involved. But I need you to find me a place to hide, someplace they won't look."

"Didn't want to get me involved? You've got to be kidding. I *am* involved. And why do you need to hide? What are you talking about?" I shouted. "Let's get out of this rain and go back to my place. We've got to talk. Now. Privately." I thought it best that I do my no-nonsense thing. Set the mood. Get to the bottom. But not out there, obviously.

Zuri insisted that we leave her car way out on the far side of the docks where it wouldn't be seen by anybody. The way she was talking, I thought for a minute that she was going to ask me to ditch it in the Solway. We got into my car, drove back, and dashed into the house, though I don't know why. We were both soaked to our bones. We pulled off our wet coats. We went upstairs. I turned on the gas fire in the front room and closed the curtains against the night. Zuri took a hot shower and then dressed in my San Francisco 49ers sweatshirt and pants, grabbed a small blanket from the bedroom, and curled up on the couch.

I poured us each a large Macallan. I couldn't settle, pacing up and down. So I took a sip and went for it. I could see she was shaken and wanted to tell all, but I had things on my mind too. I needed to know if she was a murderer before getting into London, Chantall, and standing in the rain.

"Are you wanted in Harare for murder?" I didn't know how else to ask it, and it's my way to shoot from the hip.

She didn't say anything for a minute, just hugged the blanket tighter around her and looked into the fire. I gave her time. Without taking her eyes off the fire, she softly and sadly said, "Oh, God."

Another eternity passed. Then she shook her head and looked at me. "Could you please sit down? Your pacing is making things worse. What have you heard?"

Right before my eyes, she was pulling herself together. She was one tough cookie. I kept pacing and did a quick recap of Kelly's story.

"Well, you are partly right," she said. "But there's more to it."

"My God, you shot and killed a man?"

"Yes, I did."

"Do you know what kind of shit you're in? You just became suspect numero uno here." I was shouting now.

"For God's sake, Drake, sit down and shut up and listen."

I did as she asked but kept my distance, sitting at the dining table as she began telling her story.

"You obviously know what's been happening in Zimbabwe," she said.

"Yes, but—"

"Just listen! I told you before, my family is from Highfield, southwest of Harare. My mother sent me to New York when I was eight. My father split years ago. But my younger brother and my mother stayed in Highfield. And Chantall and Nelson—their father is still a deacon in our church—Nelson came here to study and never went back.

"Things have been really bad. The stores are empty. Drake, if you could see what it used to be like when I was little, you wouldn't believe it now. Mugabe and Zanu-PF are a total nightmare. They really are bastards, you know. Anyway, last month I was visiting Mom. One day I was returning to Highfield with my brother and some of his friends. We had gone into Harare looking for food, but mostly found empty shelves. When we got to Highfield, the road was blocked, manned by four young men from Zanu-PF. They were holding baseball bats and pipes and demanded we say the party slogan. I asked which party slogan, but I knew they meant the Zanu-PF slogan. That made them angry. I tried to talk to the guy I thought was in charge, but a group of eight more youths came and said we had to wait until the base commander arrived to search our car.

"By this time lots of people had started gathering around to watch, but keeping their distance, you know? I couldn't blame them. Zanu-PF thugs are dangerous. We waited for a half hour, and the young men became more and more nervous and aggressive. They finally searched the car themselves, taking what they wanted, which wasn't much. They started to smash the windshield and the headlamps with their pipes and bats, so my brother tried to stop them. Then they turned on us and beat us. Those onlookers all just ran away. One girl was beaten savagely and blood was running down her thighs. Another girl couldn't walk when they were done with her. They were both nineteen years old, for God's sake. My brother had broken ribs and a broken hand. I got hit in the head and knocked unconscious. By the time I came to, they had left, so I drove us all to the Harare clinic. I don't know how I did it. The girl who couldn't walk stayed in the clinic, but my brother and I drove everybody else home.

"My mother was beside herself with worry. She had heard that these guys had killed five teachers in a local school that morning and were 'on patrol.' We were all damn scared. That night three of them came to our house, three of them from the roadblock, I mean,

I guess to make sure we didn't talk. We were in the living room watching TV when they broke in. They didn't say anything, just attacked us. It all happened so quickly. They beat my brother to death. I ran to the bedroom and got my dad's old gun. My mother was screaming and they started to threaten her. So I shot one of them. I had never shot a gun in my life, but I hit him in the face. I kept shooting like crazy, and the other guys ran. I wish I had killed them all. No apologies. Fucking bastards."

"Why didn't they arrest you for killing the guy?" I asked.

"They did. I thought I was dead too. I was in their filthy cell for twelve hours. But my church came up with bail. They worry about having enough food to eat, but overnight they raised the money to get me out. I owe my life to them. Chantall and Nelson's father came to get me and drove me home. I've never been so glad to see anybody in my whole life. But even then I thought it all happened a bit too easily. I mean, why would they let me out on bail at all? I had killed a Zanu-PF guy, for God's sake. I should have figured out what was happening.

"In the days that followed, we buried my brother. But as soon as I could, I was on a plane back to New Orleans. During the whole mourning period I was heartbroken and scared out of my mind.

"But what really haunted me is how they knew where we lived." I thought she'd burn a hole in the fire itself, the way she was staring into it. "Now I'm afraid I know the answer," she said.

She paused, and then reached over the arm of the couch and lifted her bag. She placed it in her lap, opened it, reached in, and pulled out a gun. She said, "This isn't the one I used in Harare. This one's better."

I stood up and shouted, "Where the hell did you get a gun?"

"Calm yourself. I live in America. They give these things out when you open a bank account."

"Is it hot?"

"No, it's not *hot*," she said scathingly. "But it's not registered either."

"How the hell did you get it here, into Britain?"

"There are ways. There are always ways," she said and put the gun back in her bag.

"So what the hell are you doing with it here in Silloth?"

"I'm sure now. Before I thought maybe I was just being paranoid, but now I have no doubt. Sekuru is looking for me with revenge on his mind. I'm not about to be killed by a bastard, and especially not that bastard."

I was beginning to think that Zuri hadn't been shaking with fear on the dock. Or if she had been, the whiskey had taken it down a few notches. At that moment I was certain that if this Sekuru guy had walked into the room, she would have shot him dead.

"Who the hell is Sekuru?" I asked, trying to keep up and stay calm.

"Sekuru. He's the father of the young man I killed. Everyone calls him that—it isn't his name, it's kind of his street title, if you know what I mean. Sekuru means 'uncle' in Shona. Kids use it for their real uncles like they do everywhere, but in Africa it's more than that. It's a significant sign of respect."

"Great. And I was worried about your part in the death of Silvestre Tolentino. Now you've got somebody's father after you. Unbelievable," I said, sitting down again.

"No, it's believable. Trust me. Zanu-PF has a long and angry reach. We didn't grow up in Zimbabwe wrapped in cotton wool. As we say in America, shit happens. Besides, this is personal. I killed his son."

It was too much for me. I got up and started pacing the floor again. "Zuri, you're going to have to explain this to me, and make it good. What in the name of sanity does this have to do with you standing in the rain at the mill? So you've been hiding out in Skinburness all this time? Jesus, I thought we had something going. You and me. Something that might go some distance. I've never met a girl like you."

"I'm sure you haven't. But listen to *you*! You're like an escapee from a Raymond Chandler novel. I don't know what to think about you either. Ace reporter from the *Union City Gazette*, for God's sake."

"Not the *Union City Gazette*. The *Fremont Argus News*. Big difference," I said, somewhat defensively.

"Right! Big difference! I apologize." Clearly she was starting to feel better.

So here's the dirt. As you know, after burying her brother, she left her mother in Chantall's care and returned to New Orleans. The first letter from her mother talked about the big funeral Zanu-PF had organized for the guy Zuri had killed, and how tense it had all been for a few days, and how the church members were bracing themselves, waiting for the repercussions that sure as shit would follow after Zuri skipped bail.

After the funeral, this guy, this Sekuru, had also disappeared from Highfield. Zuri was afraid that he might be on his way to the Big Easy to avenge his dead son. So taking a leave of absence from Loyola, where any idiot with a Google connection could find her, she booted up the computer to find somewhere to go. It turns out we both read the same website about how Silloth was the end of the world where nothing happens and no one cares. I made myself a mental note to talk to Piers about this great new idea I had for a marketing strategy for the hotel.

And, of course, now I knew I had been right. The morning after Tolentino's death, when we all knocked on Zuri's door, she was packing a gun in her Skinburness hotel robe. At least now I knew why. She didn't know where Sekuru was, but she wasn't taking any chances. And that was where Cousin Chantall came into play.

Chantall and Zuri were, obviously, cousins, but also good friends as children, like sisters, she said. They attended the same church in Highfield and grew up together until Zuri's mom packed her off to America. They kept in touch through letters and then e-mails, and saw each other when Zuri visited Highfield. Chantall was the person Zuri trusted to take care of her mother when she had to leave Highfield so abruptly.

Suddenly, it hit her. Chantall had been there in the crowd at the roadblock. The memory flashed back like an exploding supernova. What if Chantall was sympathetic toward Zanu-PF? Sure, they had e-mailed through the years and had great times whenever Zuri visited Zimbabwe, but they had also grown up apart. What Zuri didn't know about Chantall was a whole lot more than what she did know.

That was the kick, or rather several kicks to the stomach, and what got Zuri standing out in a Silloth freakin' storm at night. The more she thought about it, the more she became convinced that it was Chantall who told the Zanu-PF boys where she lived after the attack at the roadblock. Had to have been her. Chantall was Zanu-PF! That was the first kick. And Chantall's supposedly innocent visit with her brother Nelson in London, the come-on-down-for-old-time's-sake phone call, was a way of finding out where Zuri was hiding in order to give Sekuru the heads up. Kick two. Zuri told Chantall all about the Skinburness Hotel on her first day in London, even what room she was staying in, so Chantall could call. That was kick three.

Lying in bed that sleepless second night in London, Zuri had worked herself up into a frenzy, wondering if the purpose of her invitation to London was a reunion with Sekuru. The clock said

3:30 a.m. when she finally decided that she had to get out. She dressed silently, gathered her few things, and slipped out of the house, cursing the noise her engine made when she started the car. She got as far as Stoke-on-Trent before her lack of sleep caught up with her. She pulled into the next motorway service area and checked into the hotel there. Exhausted but safe, she crashed and didn't wake up until late in the afternoon. She decided to get a bite to eat, instinctively waiting for nightfall before resuming her drive north.

When she arrived in Silloth, she didn't dare go back to the Skinburness Hotel. Since she had cut out in the middle of the night, it was a sure bet that Nelson and Chantall knew their cover had been blown. She parked her car behind the docks, wandered around for a while trying to decide what to do, and eventually ended up in a shed, standing in the rain, with a single dirty light bulb as her only friend.

I poured us each another drink. I could only think this Sekuru guy was frickin' determined if he would follow her all the way up to Silloth. But I had some work to do. No fucking Zanu-PF mobster was going to hurt my girl.

16

Zuri and I were awakened in the morning when the landline in the bedroom rang. It was Piers. The Wigton fuzz would be arriving at the hotel around noon to interview Lily Henderson. Piers said they sounded more than serious. He asked if I wanted to sit in. Does Pinocchio have wooden balls? Of course I did. But first I needed to determine if Sekuru was hanging at the Skinburness Hotel.

I unloaded the whole pile of shit into Piers's lap: the killing in Harare, Zuri's trip to London, Chantall, Sekuru, the whole thing. He took it pretty well, I have to say. We agreed he would check reception to see if an African gentleman had checked in to the hotel. He would also question the staff about whether or not an African visitor had been seen in the hotel over the past few days. Let's be honest: a black African from Zimbabwe would be easy to spot in lily-white Silloth and Skinburness.

Zuri and I were clear that she couldn't return to her room, given that we didn't know the whereabouts of Sekuru. We also decided it was unwise for her to stay at my place. We had become something of an item in Gossiptown-on-the-Solway, and if Sekuru arrived in town, it wouldn't take him long to trace her to me. So sitting on the edge of the bed in my birthday suit, I gave Kelly a call, and sure as the rain falls on the good and the bad, she took Zuri in.

I met Piers in his office before the doughnut patrol arrived. I was somewhat relieved to hear that Sekuru had not checked in to the hotel. As we were agreeing that continued diligence was required, the Wigton cops arrived.

Lily Henderson was neither plain nor beautiful. She sat nicely somewhere in between. She had that porcelain-white skin some British girls have that is somehow attractive. By every account she was intelligent and good at her job. The hotel guests liked her, and she did everything Piers asked of her. She lived in one of those boxes along Skinburness Road with a girlfriend who worked at the mill. My guess, Lily was in her midthirties.

Inspector Witherspoon sat on the edge of the desk. PC Jamison took a chair to the right of the big cop, notepad resting on his knee. Lily Henderson placed her not-unattractive ass in a chair facing them. Piers stood to her left. I sat where I could watch them all.

"Miss Henderson, quite frankly I should have had you delivered to the police station in Wigton. I don't know why I'm so nice," Inspector Witherspoon began.

Lily Henderson didn't say a thing, but she looked pretty nervous. Piers just stood there, looking at Wigton's finest and his receptionist, his arms crossed over his big chest. Small cop started taking notes. Witherspoon reached into his inside uniform jacket pocket and pulled out a piece of paper. He opened it slowly, I thought melodramatically, and then handed it to Lily Henderson.

"So, Miss Henderson, what am I to make of that?" he asked.

Lily Henderson took the paper, which I saw was a handwritten letter, and just stared at it. I think she began to tear up. She definitely was not happy.

"What is it?" Piers asked quietly.

"It's a letter written by Miss Henderson to Mr. Tolentino. We found it tucked away at the back of his closet in a shoebox with a collection of other letters, and not all from you, Miss Henderson. Perhaps I should read it," Inspector Witherspoon said, taking the letter back.

Silvestre!

You fucking bastard. How dare you betray me like this. Fucking that black whore while I sit in here listening to the two of you. Sitting on the bed we make love in. How dare you betray me and with that black bitch. Send her back to where she came from! I thought we were soul mates, you fucking bastard.

I swear I'll kill you. I'll rip your fucking head off. And I'll kill that black whore for good measure.

Lily

I took in a breath. One angry Glaswegian girl. And I'd bet all my grandma's money she wasn't referring to New Orleans when she suggested Zuri go back to where she came from. What do you think? Hell yes, I was right.

"Pretty damning evidence, don't you think, Miss Henderson?"

"I didn't kill Silvestre! Are you crazy? I loved him," Lily Henderson whimpered, looking at Witherspoon and then at Piers. "You have to believe me. I would never hurt Silvestre. I love, loved, him more than myself."

"That letter doesn't sound much like love, Miss Henderson," PC Jamison said with just the hint of a smirk.

"Lily, tell them what happened. You need to explain this," said Piers gently.

They exchanged glances, and Lily's pleading face turned to resignation. "Well, I decided to surprise Silvestre when he finished work the other night. I felt we had become a little distant, so I decided to put a spark back in our relationship. I snuck into his flat about a half hour before he finished working."

"You had a key?" Inspector Witherspoon interrupted.

"The hotel has duplicate keys to everything. I took the one to Silvestre's flat and let myself in," Lily said.

"Go on," said Witherspoon.

"Well, as I said, I wanted to surprise him. I let myself in, went to the fridge, and poured myself a glass of white wine. I went to the bedroom, undressed, and sat in the chair."

"So the glass of wine on the table was yours? And the book was yours?" I interrupted.

"Mr. Ramsey, if you please," said Inspector Witherspoon, obviously annoyed.

"Sorry, but I've been wondering about that glass of wine. The glass was still a third full of white wine, and Ms. Manyika and Mr. Tolentino were drinking red," I said.

"Thank you, Mr. Ramsey," Witherspoon said to me. He then turned to Lily Henderson and said, "Well, Miss Henderson. What about it?"

"Well, yes, it was my wine and book. The plan was that I would be sitting in the bedroom, completely naked, reading a book and drinking wine, when Silvestre came in to go to bed. I have reading glasses so, you know, it would be kind of sexy and all. And I was reading *Fifty Shades of Grey*, which was kind of sexy too."

She looked around for confirmation. I smiled at her. As I said, Lily Henderson was no beauty, but neither was she a bow-wow. I mean, I'm just saying. I wouldn't mind finding her sitting naked in my bedroom sipping wine and reading a book. But *Fifty Shades of Grey!* Come on. Really? Well, anyway, I wouldn't have minded, pre-Zuri of course.

"So you were sitting naked in the bedroom, reading a book and drinking wine. Then what happened?" asked Inspector Witherspoon.

"Well, I heard the door open, and then I heard voices. Silvestre wasn't alone. He was with that Manyika woman. I just froze. What could I do? I heard Silvestre going into the kitchen and opening a bottle of wine. I heard them talking and laughing, and then I had to listen to them having sex. He was fucking that black whore and I had to listen!"

Lily was getting worked up, and a side of her that Piers had obviously not seen began to emerge. I had the feeling a damn horror show was about to play out right in front of poor, trusting Piers. I wasn't far wrong.

"How did that make you feel?" asked Inspector Witherspoon.

"How did it make me feel? How the fuck do you think it made me feel? I went to his desk and wrote that fucking letter. That's how it made me feel. I was so bloody angry and hurt. Silvestre and me were going to get married."

"Silvestre asked you to marry him?" asked Piers, surprised.

"Well, no. Not yet. But he would have. We were in love."

"What did you do next?" asked Witherspoon.

"I heard Silvestre coming toward the bedroom, so I grabbed my clothes and hid in the closet."

"You hid in the closet?" Witherspoon asked.

"Well, of course I hid in the closet. I couldn't let Silvestre see me.

My God, if he knew I was listening to him fuck that black bitch, I mean, what would he have thought?"

"Okay. What happened next?"

"She asked him for a blanket, and I heard him come in and take the one off the end of the bed. He always had that blanket folded neatly across the end of the bed. He got the blanket and went back into the sitting room. When he was gone, I opened the closet door and got dressed, but I got back into the closet as quickly as I could in case he came back for some reason. Then I just listened.

"Silvestre opened another bottle of wine, and the next thing I knew, they were arguing. I heard that bitch slap Silvestre. She must have hit him pretty hard 'cause I heard it all the way in the closet. Then the door slammed. Silvestre walked to the bathroom. I heard him swear and then turn on the water in the sink. I thought that was my chance, so I left the closet, threw the letter on the bed, and, as fast as I could, got the hell out of the flat. When I got outside, I thought I heard something, so I walked down the hall and peeked around the corner. I saw that monkey whore standing in the hall, naked as could be, getting dressed. That bitch! I backed away and sneaked out the back door of the hotel. The next day I put the key to the flat back in its place."

As I listened to Lily Henderson spit out her story in a rage of self-righteous scorn and despair, all I could think was that she had motive, truckloads of motive. And, of course, she had corroborated at least part of Zuri's story. I have to say, that brightened these strange days.

"Miss Henderson, you're a person of interest in Mr. Tolentino's death, so I advise you to stick close to home, " said Inspector Witherspoon. "But for now, you're dismissed. Go on, get out of here."

"Lily, we need you at the front desk. Can you handle it?" Piers said.

"Yes, Mr. Cullingworth," Lily said as she got up and left the room.

"Inspector Witherspoon, I'm shocked," said Piers. "Do you think Lily actually killed Silvestre?"

"To be honest, Mr. Cullingworth, I don't know. But we can't ignore that letter," Witherspoon said. "I'm sorry to say we're still waiting on the coroner's report. And, as always, there is the question of how she got out of the room if she did do it."

"Well," I said rather cautiously, simply because the thought was just forming in my head, "maybe she killed Mr. Tolentino and then hid in the front coat closet by the door."

"What? Why would she do that?" asked PC Jamison.

"Well, it is a long shot, but maybe she realized that her fingerprints were all over the place, assuming they were having an affair. So she locks the apartment up tight, hides in the front closet, and waits until someone comes looking for Mr. Tolentino. Piers, you try to enter and find the chain on. You get one of your boys to cut the chain and then you enter. She waits until you're in the back bedroom, discovering Mr. Tolentino's body, and then makes a run for it."

"But why the hell would she do that?" asked Jamison again. "It's crazy."

"Because she's smart. Because she knows that you guys can never pin the murder on her if you can't explain how she got out of a locked apartment," I said, knowing it sounded lame.

Piers was about to speak, but Inspector Witherspoon held up his hand to silence him. "Sorry, Mr. Cullingworth, but we need to go. We're late already," he said. "Mr. Ramsey, your theory is not very convincing. It's hard to see Miss Henderson hiding away in a small coat closet until someone finally came looking for Mr. Tolentino, though I guess it would explain a few things. Let's hope the coroner's report clears things up."

Yeah, let's hope. But hell's bells. Tolentino was dead, and my gut told me it was murder, so someone had to have killed him and found a way to leave a locked apartment.

17

I decided to make the rounds in Silloth to see if Sekuru had shown his face. Personally, I figured that, given his visibility, he'd keep a low profile, if he had indeed followed Zuri up to Whiteland on the Solway. But, as they say, better safe than sorry. I hit all the hotspots in Silloth—the post office, the Spar grocery store, the pub (which opened for morning coffee), old man Gartwright's shop, the newsagent, the tiny, dreary café, the baker—pretending I was looking for an African friend and wondering if he had dropped in.

After an hour and a half, I was pretty damn sure Sekuru hadn't been taking in the sights. Nonetheless, Zuri stayed with Kelly and Parker. Perhaps the tension was getting to me. While I was glad Sekuru had not appeared, I still wanted to know where the hell he was. If Zuri's imagination had been running away with her, we were doing a lot of hiding from somebody who might never show.

Zuri tried calling Chantall but only got her voice mail. She did not respond to Zuri's request for a "chat."

By the time I got back from my wander around Silloth, it was nearly two o'clock, so I hit the kitchen to prepare a late lunch. I had developed the habit of turning on the radio when I was in the kitchen, and while I was making a sandwich, this damn radio soap came on. I don't know. *The Archways* or something. It's about some farmers in some little village. I mean, you would not believe it! I gotta tell you, I've never heard so much whining and moaning and bitching from so many people in all my life, and so loudly. Apparently the natives absolutely loved this show, but as far as I was concerned, every last fucking one of them could commit mass suicide and save us from all that noise pollution. I was about to turn the damn thing off when my cell rang.

It was Piers. He had been invited to the Wigton police station that afternoon to hear the coroner's report and was asking if I wanted to come along. He laughed as he asked, knowing the answer. All I could think was, *It's about fucking time!*

I wolfed down my sandwich and drove down to the hotel to meet Piers. When I got there, Libbie and Kara were standing with Piers at the back door to their apartment. A couple of quick hugs, and then Piers and I piled into his car, which was a whole lot better than my bird-shit-covered, red, leaky demon, and headed to Wigton to get the lowdown on Silvestre Tolentino's cause of death.

I knew if the coroner had found death by poisoning, Johnny H and Lily Henderson would be in play, but so too would Zuri. And if the news of her killing a scumbag in Zimbabwe came out, she'd be up that old shit creek without that elusive paddle.

As we headed out of the village on Skinburness Road, with the Skinburness Creek hugging us to the left, Piers was quiet and clearly anxious. By the time Skinburness Creek turned into the

Great Gutter, absurdly named since it's where the creek turns into a piss poor flow, I could take the silence no longer.

"Speak to me," I said to Piers.

"Oh, nothing. Everything," he responded. "Thanks for asking Kelly to e-mail her report. But now the girls keep saying, 'I told you so.' What do I do if this gets out? The last thing the hotel needs is a lot of stories about deaths in room 217. And I do not want people to know the old vicar had some kind of incident in the hotel. He doesn't deserve that."

"Well, I'm not sure what to make of it all. Mostly I think it's a load of crap."

"You know, room 217 does have something of a reputation among the staff. And Jacklyn claims she saw the ghost in room 217."

"*The* ghost," I jumped in. "What do you mean *the* ghost? She got a name or something? You're not telling me you buy these stories."

"Of course not." Piers sighed. "But the staff are uneasy about the west wing and tend to put people in the east wing first. You know, room 217 is right down the hall from the statue. First room you come to. It's weird so many of the deaths were in that room. I wish Kelly had dug up the history of the statue too—just for historical curiosity, you understand."

"Well, your friend Silvestre didn't die in room 217. He was in his apartment and ready for love. I've never heard of anyone doing it with a ghost," I said, perhaps a little too forcefully.

That pretty much killed our conversation for a while. But as we approached Wigton, Piers said, "You know, whatever the coroner says, I'll have to let Lily go."

"Are you sure?" I asked.

"I can't have her becoming angry and telling someone to go back to where they came from. That's racist, Drake. Can't have it in a hotel receptionist, and I won't have it in my hotel," Piers said.

"No, I guess not."

The Wigton Constabulary is located on Station Road. It's an unimposing brick building with an old-fashioned, blue, lanternlike light over the front door with the word "Police" written in block white letters on all four sides. Inspector Witherspoon showed Piers and me into his office, a small, square room with a single window, two filing cabinets, a desk, and chairs for visitors. Witherspoon's desk was chaotic to say the least, but he seemed to know his way around it. The walls were gray with age. There was a large map of Cumbria on one wall and pictures of various cops on parade on another.

I asked about the photos, and Witherspoon explained there had been a parade in Wigton a number of years ago in which all the community services and institutions were on display. Apparently it had been quite a successful day. He would have gone on, but a young woman in blue entered the room, carrying an extra chair and news that the coroner had just arrived.

In short order, a middle-aged and weary-looking woman entered the office and took the third chair. Introductions all around, and then she unexcitedly but not coldly filled us in on Tolentino's death. I secretly recorded her report on the handy-dandy mini digital recorder I'd picked up on the *Fremont Argus News*. It seemed Silvestre Tolentino died of fear. Can you believe it?

Extreme stress or fear affects the part of the brain called the amygdala, which processes the emotion of fear in what is called a "vision to fear pathway." What happens is this: All kinds of chemicals and electrical impulses are set loose along nerve fibers. The brain excretes hormones, and the adrenal and pituitary glands respond to the stress. A great fear can cause massive release of both adrenaline-like nerve chemicals and stress hormones, causing an overload of the autonomic nervous system. Bottom line, the hormone adrenaline can be toxic if too much is released. It can damage the heart, lungs, liver, and kidneys. Almost all sudden deaths like Tolentino's are caused by damage to the heart.

"It's the heart that can kill you suddenly," said the coroner, stating the obvious. "The adrenaline from the nervous system affects the heart muscle cells.

"Technically, all this causes calcium channels in the cell membranes to open, and calcium rushes into the heart cells, which in turn causes the heart muscles to contract. If there is a strong enough storm of adrenaline, then calcium keeps pouring into the cells, and the heart can't relax. If the heart can't relax, the muscles and nerve tissues are overwhelmed, abnormal heart rhythms set in, and you die. The heart just shuts down. Death is quicker if the blood vessels also constrict, cutting off oxygen to the heart, which of course makes matters worse."

"Doc, are you telling us Mr. Tolentino died of fear?" I asked, because that was what we all wanted to know.

"Well, basically yes. That's the best explanation I have," she said, crossing her legs. "Mr. Tolentino didn't have a stroke, and there was no evidence of previous heart disease. While a bit overweight, he was basically a fit man. I have described what happened to his heart, and the best explanation for that is fear. Sorry if that is unsatisfactory, gentlemen."

I sat there remembering the look on Tolentino's face when I saw him lying on his bed. Fear was good enough for me. But what the hell scared him so much his heart clogged up with all kinds of shit and stopped? Being confronted by a mob assassin? Realizing the woman he just had sex with had poisoned him? Worrying that his Glaswegian love had put a hit out on him? Or realizing that Casper-the-friendly-fucking ghost was tugging on his condom?

"Nothing else?" Inspector Witherspoon asked. "No indication

of poison? Poisoning would help me make sense of a few leads I'm pursuing."

"No. No evidence of any poisoning," the coroner said. "I don't know what to tell you. Mr. Tolentino's heart was overwhelmed and stopped. Why his heart became overwhelmed, I can't say. But something frightened the life out of him."

"Or someone," Inspector Witherspoon added.

18

Back in Fremont a coroner's report that found no foul play would mean case closed, and I assumed it would be the same here in hicksville. So why did I get the feeling that Witherspoon was still tying up loose ends? Did he know Zuri had killed a man in Harare? Would he care?

When Piers and I got back to the hotel, Basil greeted us with tail-wagging fervor and the girls invited me in for lunch. Jacklyn was in the kitchen, drinking tea and reading the paper. When I entered, she gave me a big hug and asked about the coroner's report. I foolishly told her in front of Kara and Libbie. They both jumped all over it.

"I saw Kelly's report," said Jacklyn.

"You didn't show it to them?" I asked, looking at Libbie and Kara.

"No." Jacklyn smiled.

"Well, if Silvestre was frightened to death, we all know how it happened," Libbie said.

"Let it be. But why don't you show Drake the statue when we're done eating?" Jacklyn said.

"Yeah, I guess it's about time I had a look at it," I said, with as much skepticism as I could muster.

After lunch, Libbie and Kara led me up the main staircase of the hotel to the second floor. There was a corridor that ran between the west and east wings. The outer wall of the corridor was framed glass, looking out over the garden below and between the hotel wings. The inner wall was of natural stone, very attractive and warm. Along the glass wall were a number of large potted plants. Along the stone wall, four wicker chairs and tables. Overhead, the framed glass continued, forming a large skylight that ran the entire length of the corridor. As a result, it was a warm and pleasant place for guests to sit and read or talk or just wonder what it's all about.

The statue was located at the end of the corridor where it connected with the hallway leading to the rooms in the west wing. At first sight, I had to admit it was striking. The statue was of a young woman, life-size, carved out of white marble. The figure had a slender face with full lips. Her long hair fell down her back and over her right shoulder to her breast. Her left hand was over her stomach, and her right arm hung down by her side. Her left leg was set slightly forward, thus exposing it from her garment. The garment itself was a very light robe of some kind, with thin straps over her otherwise bare shoulders. Her arms and chest were also bare. The robe was almost transparent, and you could clearly see her breasts and nipples. I was slightly embarrassed, standing there staring at the statue with Kara and Libbie looking on. They, on the other hand, were totally at ease. In fact, I do believe they enjoyed my discomfort.

"Does she have a name?" I asked them both.

"No," said Libbie. "People don't like her much."

"Why's that?"

"The ghost," said Kara.

"Right, the ghost," I said, and looked at them both.

"If you don't believe us, let's make a deal," Kara said. "You stay in room 217 for five nights, and if you don't meet her by then, Libbie and I will never mention it again. At least, not until the next man is murdered in the hotel. We saw Kelly's report."

"How did you guys get ahold of that?" I asked.

"We have our ways," Libbie said. "But what about our deal?"

"Well, only if it's okay with your father," I said, assuming Piers would nuke the idea before it even got started.

To my utter surprise, he didn't. "I can't say no to my girls," he said. "And the hotel isn't exactly full. You can start tonight if you want."

Really?

I must confess, I was apprehensive, but when I saw the room, I calmed down. It was actually very nice. As you entered, the bed was slightly to the right, bedside tables with lamps on each side. To the right of the bed was a round table with two comfortable chairs next to a large window looking down on the garden. To the left of the bed was a large fireplace and an even larger mantelpiece with a shelf and mirror above it. There was a flat stone in front of the fireplace that looked as old as the hotel itself. On the right was a basket filled with wood, and to the left a fireplace set. One of those deals with a brush, shovel, and substantial poker. To the left of the fireplace was a desk, desk chair, lamp, and Internet connection. And immediately left of the door was a bathroom with a large walk-in shower. The walls were papered in a warm, uncluttered pattern. The carpet was thick. The room was great. I suddenly thought five nights holed up here wouldn't be all that bad.

I thought, foolishly it must be agreed, that Zuri could join me for the night. Nice room. Sexy girl. But, of course, even the thought was stupid, what with this Sekuru guy in the picture. Just not safe. Besides, part of the deal with Kara and Libbie was that I had to stay in room 217 by myself. They were of the opinion that the ghost would only visit if I was alone.

That night, after I had settled into the room, I lay on the bed and couldn't help imagining what it would be like if Zuri were with me. We could order room service, light the fire, and shut out the world. But all that imagining was more frustrating than enjoyable, so I set up my laptop on the desk, poured myself a whiskey from the minibar, and turned my attention to Chad Steel.

Three days had passed and no word from Rashida. Then, in the middle of an important negotiation that would land Chad Steel a bundle of coin, his communication implant signaled that there was an incoming call. He tilted his head to see the read and was relieved to discover it was Rashida. She was asking him to meet her in the southwest restricted area of the capital city. She was emphatic about not bringing backup. Chad Steel left the negotiations hanging. What was money, after all, compared to intrigue and a beautiful woman? And whenever did Chad Steel need backup?

He found Rashida standing tall against the rain and wind, in plain sight. Her hands were at her sides, but in her right hand was her laser pistol and in her left her long blade. Chad Steel approached cautiously but, of course, confidently. Before a word was spoken, they were kissing like tomorrow didn't matter.

In due course, Rashida told Chad Steel her story of killing and honor and the protection of her old mother. It was a good story, and Chad Steel knew instinctively that she was telling the truth. But truth or not, the restricted area was not the place to be telling tales of past adventures. They got into Chad Steel's air car and went to the small and humble room he had acquired for his stay on Betelgeuse.

Sitting naked together in bed, drinking the local alcoholic delight, Chad Steel learned that Rashida was being pursued by nefarious and brutal men who sought revenge on her for the killing of their clan leader. It was for this reason that she had disappeared for three days, more specifically to gather important intel. While she could handle herself in a fight, the odds were stacked against her. One woman against a diabolical clan was not good. Of course, Chad Steel would step up. But not immediately. Other demands were also being made on this, our galactic hero.

The rumors of an Agnian intrusion into the o² Gen System had grown, and the authorities of Betelgeuse had come to Chad Steel for help. Their request was simple: move into S. T.'s mansion and root out the Agnian assassin, if indeed such a brute existed. Chad Steel savored the opportunity either to prove or disprove the legend of the Agnians. His renown would grow either way. But in the secret places of his mind, he hoped the Agnian indeed did exist, for he relished the prospect of one-on-one combat with an omnipotent devil.

Though Chad Steel's brazenness was about to be tested, I realized that my eyes were heavy and my body longed for sleep. Chad Steel and the Agnian would have to wait.

That first night, I slept like a baby; well, like a baby that stirs from time to time. At one point, in the place hovering between sleep and wakefulness, I thought I heard someone walking in the hall, a kind of rustling of fabric more than footsteps. I assumed other guests had come in late. And at another point I woke up thinking the room was lighter, that someone had turned on a light or maybe the TV, but no. Must have been a dream. I got up to take a piss and was back asleep before I knew it.

I went downstairs for breakfast in the restaurant, saying good morning to the statue as I passed her in the corridor. At breakfast I asked the young woman who served me if there were many people staying in the west wing, to which she replied that, to her knowledge, I was the only one.

After breakfast I made it out of the hotel before Kara and Libbie found me, thus avoiding their interrogation. I drove home to check in at the Tilfords' and found Zuri sitting down to scrambled eggs, toast, and coffee. She asked if I had seen the ghost, and I just snorted derision. I said I wished everyone would stop referring to it as *the* ghost, as if people knew it personally. She snorted back. She was also good at derision. In fact, better than me.

That night I convinced Parker and Kelly to let me cook for us all at their place as a kind of thank-you for hiding Zuri. I cooked up one of my specialties. Fish cakes in my special tomato sauce. No freakin' hamburger meat in sight. Well, I say I cooked up a storm, but Zuri joined me in the kitchen. We sent Parker and Kelly to the living room, had a little body time, and then hit the fish cakes. I must say we made a great team, and the meal was a huge success.

After dinner, I told Parker and Kelly what I was up to. Parker was greatly amused. "I'll bet you a bottle of Macallan that you see this ghost, Drake," he said.

My gut told me some "psychology speak" was coming my way. My gut's never wrong. Nevertheless, I had to protest. "I don't believe in ghosts, and I'm betting you don't either," I said.

"Drake, hear him out," Zuri said with a laugh in her voice.

"I suggest you read up on anomalistic psychology before you embark any further on your ghost-hunting adventure," he said with a straight face. Parker liked winding me up.

"Okay, I'll bite," I said. It was often worth it to go along.

"Anomalistic psychology tries to explain the kind of phenomena you will be hunting for tonight: things like ghosts. It attempts to make sense of paranormal experiences through psychological and physical known realities. Anomalistic as in anomaly. The paranormal as anomaly. Anomalistic psychology is scientists who don't believe in ghosts trying to explain people who do. There are two possibilities: deception and self-deception. If it's deception, it means somebody else is purposely walking down that hallway and messing around with the lights. If it's self-deception, you're imagining it. Hallucinations are more common than you think. Visual or auditory, sometimes both. But there are lots of other explanations why people see ghosts. Personality disorders, weird phases of sleeping, religious obsession. Or hypnosis. Do you think anybody has tried to hypnotize you?"

I didn't respond. I knew better.

"Or suggestion. That'll be it. Come on, admit it. When you walk into room 217, isn't there a part of you that wonders whether, just maybe, the stories might be true?"

"No comment."

"Tell you what. Once you've seen the ghost, I'll analyze you and write a research paper. We'll be famous."

"I'm not going to see any ghost. There isn't any ghost," I said, with just the hint of annoyance creeping in.

"That may be true. But lots of people see them, and they're not necessarily crazy. People who have seen ghosts genuinely believe they have experienced something paranormal. It can be quite traumatizing and difficult for them to understand."

"Well, if I get traumatized, I'll know where to come," I said.

"Okay, mock me. But guess what? Belief in ghosts as supernatural agents appears in all societies. Some psychologists suggest we are predisposed to believe in the paranormal, that it's part of our evolutionary inheritance. And you, my friend, have a very active HAD," Parker countered.

"Oh, God," I moaned. "You're going to tell me what that is, aren't you?"

"It's hypersensitive agent detection, a type of instinct, and I bet yours is well developed." I again refused to comment, but, of course, he went on. "Imagine an early human being out on the savannah. He thinks he hears something. It might be his imagination, or it might be a predator coming his way. The guy who assumes it's a predator is the one who's going to survive to pass his genes on to the next generation. So now, whenever we hear something, we look for the agent that made the noise. We human beings are hypersensitive to agency. It's not crazy to think it's more than the wind whispering in the dark. So tonight when you get that feeling you are not alone, it's HAD. I suggest you have a look around," Parker said, thoroughly enjoying himself.

"Parker, you're always a font of knowledge, but I think I'll pass," I said.

"Well, if you're not interested in reading about anomalistic psychology, then I suggest you read *The Haunting of Hill House* by Shirley Jackson as a kind of primer for the evening," Parker concluded, now not attempting to hide his inner smile.

Kelly was more reserved, and I think she didn't appreciate her husband's joking. I did ask if it was normal for a good Catholic girl to believe in ghosts, and she simply said, "Who says I'm a good Catholic girl?"

I actually think Zuri enjoyed Parker's taking a shot at me.

When I went back to the hotel about nine thirty, I stopped in the bar, ostensibly for a good-night brandy. I was really looking for the mysterious African gentleman. All the faces were white, and the particular African I was looking for was not white. I popped my head in the restaurant, pretending to be looking for someone, which I guess I was. No African. I checked the billiards room and the library, and again, all clear.

I sat up in bed for quite some time reading. Perhaps foolishly, I downloaded *The Haunting of Hill House* to my Kindle. I had seen the movie years ago and it scared the shit out of me, so why I was reading the book alone in the west wing, I don't know. I may come from the mean streets of Fremont, but that doesn't mean I'm made of steel.

With these words from *The Haunting*, my evening began: "*No live organism can continue for long to exist sanely under conditions of absolute reality . . .*" Indeed! Anyway, I read until I began falling asleep, got up to take a piss, and then climbed under the covers. They were nice covers, fluffy like a comforter, what the natives call a duvet. I rolled over on my left side and then saw I hadn't pulled the curtains closed on the window, so got up again. By the time I finally settled, under my duvet as I said, I was wide awake. Nonetheless, I turned off the light and waited for the embrace of Morpheus.

At some point in the night, I rolled over onto my right side and thought I heard someone outside my door. I got up, grabbed the fancy Skinburness Hotel robe from the closet, and went to the door, thinking I'd ask the guests to keep the noise down. As I unchained and unlocked the door, I remembered the waitress saying I was the only guest in the west wing. Sure enough, when I opened the door, no one was there.

I stepped out into the hallway, looked to my left down the hall, and saw no one. I looked to my right toward the corridor and thought I saw a small wave of white light turn toward the framed glass. It was just a fleeting glimpse, like the trailing of a woman's silk robe.

I went to the corridor and looked in. No one was there, and it was dark. A light rain fell on the overhead skylight. I walked up to the glass and could see nothing outside. It was pitch-black.

I turned toward the statue, which in the dark looked both seductive and eerie, almost otherworldly. I stood for some time looking at her; precisely how long I am not sure. I must confess I did feel strangely drawn to her and at one point touched her right arm down by her side. When I touched the cold marble, the moment was broken. I laughed quietly to myself and went back to my room.

As I got into bed, I checked the clock on the bedside table. It was 2:47 a.m. I turned on the small light by the clock, telling myself I would read a bit more, but didn't even pick up my Kindle. I just wrapped myself in the duvet, and after a time fell back to sleep, not knowing that tomorrow would change everything.

19

Two incidents occurred in quick succession that caused me to take an improbable, though (I am not embarrassed to say) rather bold action. If you learn anything as a reporter for the *Fremont Argus News*, it's never to look a gift story in the mouth. Or something like that. You get my drift. Anyway, the first was important news from Piers.

I had slept late, and by the time I got up, did my business, showered, and got dressed, I had missed breakfast in the restaurant. I went looking for Piers and found him in his office. I knocked and stuck my head in the door and saw Piers and Jacklyn drinking java and talking quietly.

"Oh, Drake," Piers said. "Come in. I've got news concerning John Humphreys."

I walked into the office and took a seat next to Jacklyn. She poured me a cup of the black stuff, then, smiling, said, "See our lady ghost last night?"

"No, I did not!" I said, sipping my joe.

"The girls will be disappointed," she said.

Ignoring her, I turned to Piers sitting behind his big desk and asked, "So what's the news on Johnny H?"

"Not much, I'm afraid," Piers said, getting up and pulling his chair around the desk to sit with Jacklyn and me. "The police have decided that that inquiry is a dead end. As they said, he was in New York the night Silvestre died, and they can find no evidence that Mr. Humphreys sent someone to collect on Silvestre's debt."

"What about the gambling debts?" I asked.

"Well, it's true Silvestre owed Humphreys quite a lot, but it was all legal and aboveboard. Silvestre was paying him back. Why would Humphreys kill Silvestre when the man owed him money and was paying it back? It doesn't make sense."

"So Johnny H is in the clear," I said, almost to myself. "Is the case closed then? What about Zuri?"

"I don't know. Inspector Witherspoon didn't say, but I wouldn't be surprised. I told you to be careful there," Piers said.

"Too late for that, my friend. I'm in deep and don't want to dig myself out," I said.

"Good for you," Jacklyn said.

"Hey, good for me. But what about your receptionist? She had motive up the wazoo," I said.

"Well, on that you're right, and I assume that Lily must be the second of the couple of leads," Piers said. "We had to let her go, you know. It's a shame, because she was really very good at her job."

"How about one second chance?" I asked. Piers just looked at me askance.

So incident one, the news about Johnny H, got the ball rolling, though I didn't know it at the time. After we finished our coffee, I headed home, and before I could even get in the door, Kelly was calling me from her upstairs window. She asked me to come in, as it turned out for more coffee and more news.

Zuri poured me a cup as we sat around the kitchen table. They asked about the previous night, and I came clean about the noise and … and whatever it was I saw, or didn't see, more likely. I also told them about Johnny H being let off his leash. These two bits of information evoked secretive glances between Kelly and Zuri, and I guessed I was in for a surprise.

"Well, that's good then," Kelly said, "because I've shown more initiative."

"Now what have you done?" I asked, looking at her with more than a little anxiety.

"Hear her out, Drake, before you go all ballistic," Zuri said.

"I've arranged for you to meet with Sybil Fielding," said Kelly.

"What? Who the hell is Sybil Fielding?" I said, a little too loudly.

"Sybil Fielding! The Fielding family who gave the statue to the Skinburness. You remember," Kelly said.

I thought for a moment, and of course it came back to me. I'm a reporter after all. "Why the hell did you do that? What's the point?" I said, looking from one to the other.

"Well, I think it's a good idea. You just said you saw something last night—"

"No!" I interrupted Kelly. "I said I thought I *might* have seen something. It was probably a play of light coming through the skylight in the corridor."

"What light? It rained all last night," said Zuri. I sighed.

"And," Kelly went on, "Johnny H has been cleared. We know Zuri had nothing to do with Silvestre's death."

"Thanks," said Zuri, putting her hand on Kelly's.

"Are you both forgetting about Lily Henderson?" I asked. "She is one angry, scorned woman. Did you know she was in the bedroom while you and the Spaniard were getting it on?" I said, looking at Zuri. "After you ran out of the apartment, Silvestre went into the bathroom to wash the blood off his face where you hit him, and Lily Henderson ran out after you. She saw you getting dressed in the hall."

Zuri sat back in her chair with a look of amazement on her face. "No, I didn't know," she said quietly. "That's horrible. I really wish you hadn't told me that. But do you think she went back in and killed Silvestre?"

"How?" Kelly asked. "You think she scared him to death? Silvestre? Jacklyn told me about the coroner's report. The poor man was frightened to death. The room was locked up tight. No one could enter or leave, and yet Silvestre is dead. How did Lily kill Silvestre, lock the door, put the chain on, and also leave? It's not possible. Once we determine what is impossible, what remains can only be the truth, no matter how improbable."

"You're not suggesting ..." I started.

"She's not suggesting anything," Zuri said. "But what harm will it do to speak to Sybil Fielding?"

"Drake, the statue is mixed up in this in some way. I can feel it," Kelly said.

"You can *feel* it," I said sarcastically.

"Yes," Kelly said matter-of-factly. "Besides, it will do you no harm to get out of here for a couple of days. Zuri is safe with us. I booked you on a train tomorrow morning."

I just sighed and held my head in my hands. "What the hell," I said, defeated.

So incident two, a train ticket to London, sent the ball rolling even farther, the ball being me, of course.

20

Kelly dropped me in Carlisle to catch the train to London, assuring me she would take care of Zuri.

"Keep an eye out for Sekuru," I said.

"Drake, get out of the car," she said, giving me a shove.

At the station, I bought a tuna baguette and a Coke, a real Coke, mind you, not that diet shit. I jammed the baguette and Coke into my bag, found a store that sold newspapers, and bought a paper and a trashy novella called *Alien Love* for the ride south. I figured if the story sucked, it was at least short.

About halfway to London, the train stopped in the middle of nowhere, which is never good news. It took forty-five minutes for the conductor to tell us that the engine had died and a replacement was on the way. Two old guys sitting across the aisle from me got all philosophical about it.

"Well, these things happen," said one.

"Yup, nothing to be done," said the other.

I looked at them, more than annoyed, and said, "Bet you wouldn't be so calm about this if we were in a plane at forty thousand feet." That shut them up.

I was annoyed because the delay meant I would be stuck in London longer than I had planned. I couldn't go banging on old lady Sybil Fielding's door after nine. She was ancient. Just not right.

So, when we got in to Euston, I got myself a room in the Premier Inn just a stone's throw from the station. I gotta say the room was more expensive than the big guy on TV had me believing it would be for a hotel chain. Fortunately, I like the color purple. Honestly. Everything in the room was purple. The walls, curtains, bedspread, carpet, towels. All purple.

I hung up my shirts, did my business, and then went down to the bar to see what was happening. I ordered a Cuba Libre and took a small table by the front window looking out on Euston Road. I opened my newspaper and, pretending not to care about how the bankers and their politicians were stealing our money, cased the joint.

Behind me and to my right were four booths. One was occupied by two couples in their midthirties. At another sat a cherubic-looking man with black skin and white hair who was chatting up one of the waiters. The others were empty. In front of me was the bar, the door to Euston Road, and the hotel's restaurant. Euston Road was popping, the streetlights shining off the rain-drenched street and sidewalk, people bent against the drizzle.

I went up to the bar and asked the slender brunette for another Libre and then casually asked for directions to Hampstead. I knew the way, of course, but I thought asking for help would be a good icebreaker. It wasn't. Before I knew it, I was back to the table with my Libre and tube directions to Hampstead that I didn't need. I hid my face in the paper.

And then, nothing happened. I guess the Premier Inn wasn't the place to look for a little action. Mind you, I wasn't thinking of anything dubious, given my relationship, or whatever it was, with Zuri. But Silloth was an action-free zone, so who could blame me for wanting a little flirtation before heading off to bed by myself? I contemplated going out in the rain to find what I had told myself I needed, but instead had a third Cuban and then went up to my purple room and fell asleep with the TV on.

In the morning I went down to the lobby, picked up a complimentary paper, and went to the restaurant for my full English and black coffee. Both were damn good. I lingered over my paper with a couple more javas and then went up to my room to call the ancient but willing Sybil Fielding.

Kelly had done the groundwork, of course. I knew she was ninety-three years old and lived by herself in a big family house, probably worth a fortune, in Hampstead. She had served as a nurse during the war and later in life took over the family business, successfully and decisively. Kelly had also assured me that Sybil Fielding was more than willing to meet, and it proved to be true. I was surprised when she answered the phone herself. We agreed on an eleven o'clock meeting. I packed my bag, paid my bill, and headed up the Northern Line to Hampstead.

When I escaped from the underground into Hampstead, yesterday's rain was nowhere to be seen. I wandered around with my bag over my shoulder and finally settled in a café for yet another coffee. I sat in the front window and watched the rich people do their rich people things, and finally got up and asked the guy who made my latte how to get to the Fielding place. At precisely eleven o'clock I was knocking on the old broad's door.

A young woman with an Eastern European accent opened the door and greeted me. I introduced myself. She told me Mrs. Fielding was waiting for me in what turned out to be the very large rear living room. Sybil Fielding was sitting in a straight-backed chair by a large window looking out over the garden. She didn't get up when I entered the room, but smiled broadly and said, "You must be Mr. Ramsey."

"Yes, ma'am," I said. "I'm Drake Ramsey. People call me Drake."

"Well, come over here and sit down. Renia, would you get us some coffee? Coffee acceptable, Mr. Ramsey?"

"Yes; that would be great," I said, wondering how much java I could pour in before needing to take a leak. As Renia left the room, I realized the big "window" was actually a sliding glass door.

Sybil Fielding must have seen the lightbulb go on in my head because she said, "Yes, it's nice in the summer when we can open it. I love the feeling of the summer air and the house being opened to the garden."

Even for this time of year, the backyard and garden were beautifully kept, and though it was obvious Sybil Fielding was in excellent shape for a ninety-three-year-old woman, I bet she didn't work the garden herself. We made more small talk, mostly about me being a Yank; that's what she called me, a Yank. Renia came back with the coffee, pulled a small table between us, and placed a coffeepot and two cups in front of us. Sybil Fielding leaned over. "Milk and sugar, Mr. Ramsey?"

"No. I take it black, and do call me Drake."

"As you wish, Mr. Ramsey."

She poured the coffee, and we both sipped carefully, looking out at the garden. When I thought it appropriate, I put my cup down and said, "Miss Fielding, I'm very grateful you agreed to see me."

"My pleasure. I was intrigued when that nice Mrs. Tilford contacted me, and for such a surprising reason. I haven't thought of that sculpture in years. Well, to be honest, I never think about it.

My grandfather, Montgomery Fielding, gave it to the Skinburness Hotel thirty-seven years before I was born. He was only twenty-six at the time, but his parents had died, and apparently he never liked her—the statue I mean."

I reached into my bag and pulled out my iPad that held photos I had taken of the statue. "Forgive me, but can we make sure we're talking about the same statue? I've brought along a few photos."

"Yes, let's. I too have some photographs. I put them on the bookshelf over there. Do you mind?"

"Not at all," I said. I got up and handed her the iPad. I went over to the shelf and picked up the photos. It was clear as a full moon on a cloudless night that we were looking at the same sculpture.

"Mr. Ramsey, I'm afraid you will need to help me with this device. I haven't gone digital, as I think they say."

"Yes, of course. I'm sorry," I said and knelt down beside her chair to show her the pictures.

She handed me back my iPad and said, "That is certainly her."

"Do you know why your grandfather gave the sculpture to the Skinburness Hotel?" I said as I returned to my chair.

"Well, as I said, he wasn't fond of her. Of course, I never spoke to him about it, but one day I found the photographs you are now holding and asked my grandmother about them. I think I must have been around twelve or thirteen years old. Grandmother became tense; I remember that quite clearly. Yes, Mr. Ramsey, I'm old, but I'm still blessed with an excellent memory."

I think I actually blushed. She was reading my mind. Recovering, I asked, "What did she say about it?"

"Well, at first not much, just that it was in the house when she came here as a young bride and that Grandfather gave it to the hotel. When I was older, perhaps twenty, the issue of the sculpture came up again. It was during the war, and we were very worried about the

128

bombing. You know, a bomb fell not a mile from here, and many families were taking their art treasures to relatives and friends in the countryside for safekeeping. My great-grandfather had been a great collector of art from the Continent, and some of it was quite valuable.

"One day when I was home on leave, my grandmother asked me if I would help her make lists and put all the papers in order. I came across the bill of sale for the statue with a photo I hadn't seen before. The statue was so beautiful; I couldn't understand why my grandfather would give it away when it was part of the family collection. So I asked her again. This time she refused to speak about it at all. The next day she gave me one of Grandfather's journals and told me to read it, and after that she never said another word about it. There we were, German bombs every night, but even so, what I read struck me as very dramatic. I can't imagine what it will sound like to you, Mr. Ramsey."

"Would it be too much to ask to see the journal myself?" I asked.

"I'm afraid that's impossible. Grandmother had all Grandfather's journals buried with her when she died. I was never quite sure why, but it was explicitly written into her will. I'm afraid you will have to rely on my memory," she said with a twinkle and sly smile.

Apparently you didn't mess with Sybil Fielding. She poured us another cup of coffee and continued.

"Grandfather thought the sculpture was bad luck, perhaps even sinister. It seems he was both attracted to her and frightened by her. You've seen her. You know. In any event, Grandfather wrote that she was *extremely* beautiful but that he always felt uneasy when he walked past her. Which he did often, Mr. Ramsey. She stood on the small landing where the stairs turn to the right and continue to the first floor. You no doubt saw the large staircase when you came in. I believe she stood there from the day she was brought into the house. I will ask Renia to show you the place after we are done speaking."

"I would like that, thank you."

She sipped her coffee, set the cup back in the saucer, folded her hands in her lap, and went on. "Grandfather wrote in his journal about a death in the house, this very house. One of his colleagues had come to dinner, and they ended up talking and drinking brandy into the early hours. He was a single man, and instead of going home stayed in the guest room. That was not unusual. Apparently Grandfather was quite the social entertainer in his youth. In the morning, Grandfather's guest did not appear for breakfast, and after some time Grandfather sent a servant up to waken him. I'm sure you have guessed what the servant found. The gentleman was found lying on top of the bedsheets, stark naked and dead. He was looking straight up at the ceiling with the fear of death imprinted on his face."

Sybil Fielding paused and looked out the window, I assumed to compose herself. "I do not like the coming of winter, Mr. Ramsey. The garden looks so cold, or perhaps I'm seeing it colder than it really is. Anticipating the cold, if you will."

I looked at the garden and didn't say anything. I'd been here before and knew that my source just needed a little time to get over the hump before sharing the more difficult and pertinent part of her story. It would come. She wanted to tell it. So I sat silently and waited.

"Here's where it gets really interesting, Mr. Ramsey," she said, still looking out the sliding door. "Apparently, one of the servants had heard the bell ring for the guest bedroom, or thought he had. He got out of bed, dressed, and just as he reached the top of the stairs and turned to go down the hall to the bedroom, he saw a woman dressed in white entering the room. He assumed that the bell had been a mistake and that Grandfather's guest had a woman caller. He was a good servant and went back to his bed, asking no questions and disturbing no one. The next day the police questioned the staff, and he told his story. When pushed to describe in more detail what the woman looked like, he said she looked something like the statue on the landing. Grandfather became angry, scolding the servant for his outrageous story, and actually dismissed the poor man. After all, it was hardly right for a servant to suggest that an important guest of the house had arranged for a woman to visit him in the middle of the night, unbeknownst to anybody. Wouldn't you agree that that is quite preposterous? In due course the death was declared natural, and there the story almost ended."

"Almost?"

"Yes. Grandfather would never speak of the death and the woman again, though my father always maintained that he was hiding something. In any event, as is the wont of people, gossip had it that the woman in white and the sculpture were somehow linked."

"What do you think? I mean, how could they be linked?"

"Just an old story, I presume. One to scare children before they go to sleep."

"But your grandfather got rid of the statue, did he not?"

"That he indeed did. He surely did."

We both fell silent. Renia popped her head around the door, and when Sybil Fielding did not respond, she left.

"Just two more questions, Mrs. Fielding, if I may."

"Certainly," she said, but I could see she was tiring.

"Why the Skinburness Hotel?" I asked.

"The Fielding and the Banks families did quite a bit of business together in those days. The hotel was built by Edwin Hodge Banks of Highmoor House in Wigton. Edwin Banks had seen the sculpture when visiting here and, according to Grandfather's journal, had fallen in love with her. Imagine that. Falling in love with a piece of marble. Anyway, Edwin Banks's son made an approach to my family to say how nice it would be to find a place for her in the new hotel. Grandfather was more than happy to get rid of the thing, and she moved north."

"And where did your great-grandfather get the statue?"

"Ah, now. I thought you might ask that, so I went back to that list I made all those years ago during the war. My family keeps good records, you see. The statue came from Prague."

"Prague!" I interrupted.

"Yes. It had been purchased from the sculptor and remained in the family of one of my great-grandfather's business associates there."

"Do you know the name of the sculptor?" I asked, holding back my excitement.

"His surname was Černý. The bill of sale is dated 1870, but aside from the photographs and the sales note, nothing of that story remains. It's the best I can do." And with that the interview came to an end.

I hightailed it to the underground and caught the Northern Line back to Euston Station and the Premier Inn. I had a plan.

21

I was welcomed back to the Premier Inn by a beautiful young redhead who made me wish I were fifteen years younger and ten pounds lighter. Once checked back into my purple room, I called Kelly and gave her the lowdown on my interview with Sybil Fielding. I told her to chase down the dead and buried sculptor Černý and to get as much information about him and his work as she could. She took to the challenge like a duck to water.

"And make it snappy," I said. "London's nice, but it rains down here too, and I'm thinking I may have to make my way to Prague."

"You're thinking about going to Prague?" she said, slightly surprised.

"You go where the story leads, Kelly. Or at least that's what we do on the *Fremont Argus News*. That's the game, and if you don't want to play, get another job."

"Yeah, right," she said as she laughed.

I decided to hit the streets of London. The sun was still shining and that certainly wouldn't last forever. I thought getting out would lift my spirits. But before I left the room, I checked on flights to Prague. I was counting on Kelly coming back with the goods, and I wanted to stay ahead of the game.

I found a fairly cheap British Airways flight out of Heathrow, ditching the easyJet option because I didn't want to make the trip to Gatwick. It was a close call because I knew I had to watch my expenses. Dear Granny might start rolling over. If I didn't take care, before long I'd be rubbing two quarters together, hoping they'd have baby nickels and dimes.

I navigated my way to Balans on Old Compton Street. Both the restaurant and the street are gay as gay can be, which was a relief after the homogeneity of Same-Old-Same-Old-Town, my home up north. I had been there once before, many years ago, and I remembered that they made excellent eggs Benedict. I bought several newspapers along the way, wanting to get a feel for what was going on in the big, bad world after living in my news-free zone. It all made for a good afternoon, and yes, the eggs Benedict were still to die for.

I lingered over the evidence smeared across my plate, moving from coffee to a beer. Late afternoon had snuck up on me. I was sitting at a small table in the corner by the front window, watching the people walk up and down the street. It felt like I had been liberated from the confines of my small, bent-over town.

An older couple, I guess in their midsixties, walked up and looked at the menu in the window. Obviously Americans, they looked like George and Martha from Iowa. They came in, took a table, and only then looked around them. When they saw where they were, surrounded by gay men and lesbians, a look of shock came over their faces. Not disgust or anything like that, but a look of "what the hell are we doing in here?" They got up and left, not in a mad rush, but not slowly either. Hell, it would make for a good story back home in Iowa.

My time in London sort of disappeared on me. Purple room, walks on crowded streets, restaurants, newspapers, and rain. The damn rain had returned. I didn't talk to anyone except the redhead in reception. But on the third day Kelly called, and she had come up trumps. Good old Kelly.

She had discovered, or was at least pretty sure, that Černý, whose first name turned out to be Cénék, did shape a figure like our lady in the Skinburness. And, believe it or not, Kelly found a professor type who was not only willing to meet with me to talk about Cénék Černý, but actually offered to put me up in his apartment for a couple of days. My dear grandma must have sent him a spirit message.

My expert was called Dr. Jaroslav Raich, a prof at Charles University. Kelly said that he called himself a narratologist, a mythologist, an historian, and a lover of art. Not sure what the hell all that meant, but he also said he was familiar with Cénék Černý, and that was good enough for me.

I exchanged e-mails with Dr. Raich, bought that flight to Prague, and readied myself for a couple of stuffy days with a narratologist/ mythologist in a stuffy apartment with what I assumed would be his equally stuffy wife. No one said the reporter's calling was easy.

From the Václav Havel Airport, I took the metro as far as it would go and followed Dr. Raich's directions toward the place he proposed to meet me. With time to spare, I entered a Prague park, my leather bag over my shoulder, and began looking for a bench. I spotted one across the grass and so stepped off the paved walkway to take the shortest route to my rest.

Just as I stepped onto the grass, an old man shouted at me. I stopped, turned, and looked at him. He was one angry old guy.

In righteous indignation he yelled again, this time pointing at the pathway and then at the grass in exaggerated gestures. At first I didn't understand what he was so worked up about, but then it dawned on me. The old man, in a moment of civic pride, was telling me not to walk on the grass.

I looked at the long way around to the empty bench, and then at the grass, only to discover that there really wasn't much grass at all. It was just a patch of weeds, dirt, and dog shit. I looked again at the old man.

"You're kidding," I yelled back.

Of course the old bastard didn't understand me, and he started shouting again, this time waving his cane in the air. I stood there for a second, looked down, and shook my head. *Drake*, I said to myself, *it's his damn city*. I took the long way around.

When I got to the bench, I sat down and looked back at the old man. Bless the old bastard, he sat triumphant, his companions nodding their approval at his victory. We sat and stared at each other across the dirt and shit. A dog ran by, stopped, and shit right there between us. I laughed. The old man growled. I got up and walked behind the bench, found a bush, and pissed in the dirt. I turned and tucked in my shirt and zipped up my pants. The old man got up, spit on the ground, and walked away.

It was a good place to wait, a small island, Slovanský ostrov on the Vltava River. Raich and his wife lived in a large flat on Pstrossova, which was a short walk away near the city center.

Dr. Raich arrived about three in the afternoon. He walked right up to me. I guess I looked like I didn't belong. I stood up, reached out my hand, and said, "Dr. Raich?" He smiled, so I continued, "Hi. I'm Drake. Drake Ramsey. People call me Drake."

"It's nice to meet you, Drake. And please, you must call me Jaroslav," he said.

We walked to his apartment, which was in a huge old building. We entered a dark and dirty hallway through large wooden doors. Everything was covered in plaster dust. He explained in his very good English that the entire building was being rewired. At the end of the hall were a large staircase and a small elevator that belonged in an old movie. We took the elevator to the third floor. I watched the building pass through the iron grid of the elevator's door. Everything I saw seemed ancient, though I learned later the building itself was only eighty years old.

His flat was large with high ceilings. On the walls were unusual works of art. Plants were placed here and there. There was a stereo with turntable, but no CD player. A small television (black and white!) sat on a bookshelf. Books and vinyl records were all over the place. Dr. Raich might have been younger than I anticipated, but he was still somewhat of an eccentric. The apartment looked clean, but he would get no awards for neatness. Tall, narrow-windowed doors opened onto very small balconies that looked down onto Pstrossova.

The room in which I stayed was also tall and narrow—everything was tall and narrow—and very comfortable. I dropped my bag on the bed and stepped out onto my small balcony. Below me, Pstrossova was busy and noisy. Across the street was a woman sitting by her window, staring at me. She ended up being my companion during my time in that room. She never seemed to change out of her light pink robe. Age had got to her. She always had a cigarette in her mouth. It seemed she never left her window. I'd bet she didn't miss a thing on the street below.

And God knew there was plenty to look at. People walking here and there, cars and trucks rushing up and down. There was an accident on the second morning of my stay. I rushed out onto the balcony when I heard the crash, and there she was, watching the entire scene. She saw me and, acknowledging our relationship, laughed, pointing to the cars and the people arguing below. I laughed too and shook my head. It felt good being out of dysfunctional, waterlogged Silloth. I didn't think the people in Silloth would have the ingenuity to run into each other.

Anyway, Dr. Raich gave me about fifteen minutes to put my bag down and run some water over my face, and then he took me around the corner to the U Flekū. He told me, with not a little pride, that the U Flekū had been brewing and serving beer there since 1499. Gotta say, I was impressed.

We entered and walked through the building into a large central courtyard located at Křemencova 11. All around the patio were trees, tiled roofs, large picnic-like tables, waiters rushing around with huge glasses of beer. On the edge of a roof sat a gray cat quietly observing everyone. We drank Flekovsky Cerny Lezok 13, which was a damn good, rich, dark beer brewed on the grounds.

Dr. Raich was one of the most pleasant people I have met. Not the stuffy old fart I had anticipated. He was tall, slender, dressed in jeans and a loose blue shirt. He walked with confidence. There was always a smile on his face, and he seemed permanently excited.

That night, after his wife, Šárka, had returned from work at the Italian embassy, he made a large omelet and we shared a quiet dinner. Šárka was an intelligent, pretty, slender delight. She too had a smile that could brighten up a gloomy day. After we had finished our meal and cleared the table (dishes placed in the sink for later), a friend from the floor above came down for Turkish coffee, slivovitz, and conversation. This upstairs friend was a cellist and seemingly passionate about everything. He insisted I go upstairs to his apartment and listen to him play, and so I did. On his wall was a large Jesus figure, crucified, but with no cross behind it. It was Jesus crucified in midair. Yes, there had been a cross at one time, but it had been missing for ages. In fact, he had never seen it. But I'm getting ahead of myself.

In the morning, I woke early, greeted the old lady across the street, showered, shaved, shit, and then left with Dr. Raich. He bought a copy of *Lidove Noviny* along our way to the Slavia Café for coffee. Couldn't get much better than the Slavia. It was located on the corner of Národní Street and Smetanovo nábřeží, opposite the National Theater. We got a seat by the window, and I sat there looking out at the Vltava River and Prague Castle. It was so beautiful I almost forgot why I had come.

But as good as it felt to have escaped the rain-drenched asylum we affectionately called Silloth, I was there for information, information Dr. Raich was eager to share. So as we sat over coffee, I pulled out my digital recorder, checking to make sure I wasn't about to record over my interview with Sybil Fielding, and we got down to business.

"So, Drake, you have an interest in Cének Černý," Dr. Raich said, talking over his cup.

"Well, not so much Cének Černý but a sculpture I think he did," I said as I retrieved my iPad from my bag. I juiced it up and found the photos of the statue in the Skinburness Hotel. I handed the iPad to Raich and watched as he swiped through the lot, taking his time over each and every photo. I sat silently looking at his face, not the Prague Castle. Tourist time was over.

"Where did you get these photos?"

"I took them myself. The statue is sitting in a five-star hotel in the back of beyond in northern England. The place is called the Skinburness Hotel."

He looked at me, genuinely surprised. "She is called *The Woman in White Marble*, and indeed was sculpted by Cének Černý. She is beautiful, don't you think?"

139

"Yes, very. Almost eerily so."

"I wish I could see her."

"Well, as I said, she's sitting in a corridor in the hotel and isn't going anywhere. Unfortunately, you would have to come to Silloth to have a look."

"Sitting in a corridor. Incredible," he almost whispered. And then suddenly he sat up straight, took another drink of coffee, and started to talk somewhat rapidly. "To the best of our knowledge, *The Woman in White Marble* was completed around 1765."

"Last week I met with a Sybil Fielding in London. She told me her great-grandfather had bought the statue in 1870 and that her grandfather gifted the thing to the Skinburness Hotel in 1885. That's 105 years in between. Do you know where the statue was for that time?"

"Unfortunately, I'm not so knowledgeable about *The Woman in White Marble*'s travels, though she apparently was in Černý's house when the house was sold to a wealthy Prague family after Černý's death. However, I can tell you about the stories surrounding her and her creator."

"I'm all ears," I said, sliding my recorder a bit closer to him.

"It's not a pleasant story. Legend has it that Černý used one of his servants, a young woman, to pose for the sculpture. During the months he worked on the marble, he ... well, some say he fell in love with the model, and others say he became sexually obsessed with her. Take your pick, but whether love or obsession, the story doesn't have a happy ending."

He paused and took a sip of coffee and then a good swallow of water. I was starting to feel uncomfortable. I don't know what I had expected to hear, why I really had come all the way to Prague and crashed in this nice man's apartment. But as he talked, I remembered my strong reaction when I first saw the statue. She was, indeed, beautiful, and she somehow pulled you in. You couldn't help but stare at her. You wanted to reach out and touch her, as I did that night after everyone had gone to bed. I remember standing there in the dark, becoming aroused before returning to my room. The memory wasn't pleasant, and sitting in the Slavia Café by the Vltava River on a sunny morning, I was more than pleased that Dr. Raich couldn't read minds.

"The legend has it that when he finished the sculpture, he had it placed in his bedroom. He demanded the young model come to his bed at night, where, of course, he had sexual intercourse with her. Love or obsession, the legends never indicate she reciprocated with either. The image you get is of a powerful man forcing a young and vulnerable woman to have sexual relations.

"While that is unpleasant, it gets worse. Things turned violent. There are various versions of what happened, but they all say about the same thing. Černý became more and more physical, eventually choking and striking her during intercourse. Essentially he would rape her while looking at *The Woman in White Marble*. Then one night, as the story goes, at the point of climax, he took a knife off the nightstand and cut her throat. He was found the next morning still lying beside her, both of them covered in her blood."

"Shit," I whispered, more to myself than to Dr. Raich.

"Yes. Shit about sums it up," he said. "Of course the murder itself was fairly well documented. Černý was found in bed with his dead model. He was arrested and sentenced. So, the murder you can read about. The rest is the stuff of legends that grew up around the case. The model herself remained unidentified in both the accounts of the murder and the legends. All we know is she was young, vulnerable, and very beautiful. Of course, some versions of the legend insist she possessed him and was responsible for her own rape and murder. No surprise there. We still blame women for the violence of men. Other versions have it that Černý was evil or demonic or the devil himself. Again, no surprise. It is often the case that we explain the brutality and violence—yes, the evil of human beings by evoking supernatural powers. More common today, we turn to psychology for our explanations. In my opinion, we just can't face the fact that there is nothing inhuman about human depravity."

For a moment it seemed as though Dr. Raich had finished. He called the waiter over once again—the man liked muddy coffee— and looked out over the Vltava. I, of course, wanted more, but I wasn't about to tell this academic that some of my friends thought there was a beautiful, young female ghost running around the Skinburness Hotel, getting even. So I simply said, "Jaroslav, is that all? No more to the legends of *The Woman in White Marble*?"

"Goodness no, there is much more, but let me get another coffee. For you?" I nodded and we waited for the coffee to arrive. As we waited, he said, "Will your little magic machine there run out of space?"

At first I didn't know what he meant, but then he tapped the recorder with his index finger. "Oh! No. You could talk for a year and it would be fine."

"Well, it won't take a year," he said as our coffee arrived. He continued.

"From here things get metaphysical or even mystical. Černý was imprisoned for a number of years but was eventually released. It's said that he became a recluse, never leaving his house. Upon his death, the house and its contents were sold to a powerful and wealthy Prague gentleman. He had *The Woman in White Marble* moved from the master bedroom to the large entrance hall of the house. I imagine she stood there until traveling to London.

"Anyway, there were two more deaths in that house over the years, though neither violent like the first. Again, you can find reports for both. The two deaths, though years apart, were surprisingly similar. Both involved the death of a man. In both the men were found on the bed, completely naked. Both were looking up at the ceiling. There were no signs of violence on the bodies or in the room. Both deaths were attributed to natural causes. But intriguingly, both men were described as having a look of fear etched in their faces. It's this last factoid that I believe gave rise to the stories."

Here we go, I thought to myself.

"Legend has it that when the young model was murdered by Černý, her spirit remained earthbound due to the violent nature of her death. As you know, the notion of the dead being trapped on earth due to the nature of their deaths, or of some reluctance on the part of the spirit to depart, is part of the prevailing modern mythology of death—along with, of course, the spirit rising toward the light, the sound of beautiful music, and the greetings by deceased loved ones.

"In our case, it is said that the young woman's spirit chooses to reside in the marble sculpture, to which she returns after roaming the house through the night. And again, given her horrible death at the hands of an evil man, when the opportunity presents itself, she exacts revenge on men by drawing the life essence from their bodies after luring them to bed with the promise of sexual congress. Thus the look of fear on the men's faces. The legend would have it that the men die of fear as she draws the life from them. How she does this is never articulated, and it doesn't need to be. The story is first and foremost about the spirit of a young woman tormented in life and in death, shackled to our earthly existence as she was to her tormentor, roaming alone at night until she has the opportunity to try to balance the spiritual and moral accounts of her short life.

"So, Drake. Why did you *really* come to Prague?" And with that, he leaned back in his chair.

22

Dr. Raich asked me to be his guest for a couple of days, so he could "show me all that a good tourist should see and a whole lot of what they shouldn't." I admit it was tempting, but only for a minute. I'd been calling Zuri each day since training it down to London, but I didn't like being away from her with everything going on and no sight of Sekuru. So we went back to Dr. Raich's place, I packed my bag, and he drove me to the airport.

On the flight back to London, I couldn't stop thinking about *The Woman in White Marble*. I kept saying to myself, *For God's sake, Drake, get a grip. This is all utter nonsense.* Unfortunately, my montra didn't ease my foreboding. I was beginning to think that perhaps I actually had seen a ghost, and one that killed men.

Okay. I know what you're thinking. *Mantra*, not *montra*, you idiot. But you couldn't be more wrong. What I needed was a montra, a little something I picked up while doing a story on the Kurdish community in Fremont and Union City—and by the way, a big story for the *Fremont Argus News*, I'm not too humble to admit. *Montra* is from the Pahli word *mahantra*, which means protection. Its origin is from the Kurdish world *pala*, which means to take refuge under someone's protection. In other words, I wanted protection, not some silly-ass meditation mantra. Om, indeed! A montra is serious business. *For God's sake, Drake, get a grip. This is all utter nonsense.* I'd have to keep working on it.

I took a taxi from Heathrow to Euston and caught the first train north to Carlisle. Unfortunately, by the time I got to Carlisle it was too damn late to ask Kelly to come get me, so we arranged for her to pick me up early the next morning. I couldn't believe I wanted to get back to Silloth so badly! I couldn't sleep that night for worrying about Zuri.

On the drive from Carlisle to Silloth, I played the recording of my interview with Raich. Kelly was silent throughout. His last words sounded even more tragic on the recording: *The story is first and foremost about the spirit of a young woman tormented in life and in death, shackled to our earthly existence as she was to her tormentor, roaming alone at night until she has the opportunity to try to balance the spiritual and moral accounts of her short life.* Upon hearing those words, Kelly just looked at me. I'm sure we were both thinking the same thing, but neither of us said anything.

Finally, Kelly broke the silence. "We need to decide what to do about Zuri," she said. "She's great, but she can't stay with us forever. We've got to settle this thing with Sekuru."

Kelly was, of course, right, so I pushed *The Woman in White Marble* out of my mind. "You're right, and thanks for letting her stay with you guys. When we get back, we'll all think it through."

Back at Kelly's house, we sat around the kitchen table, including Parker, who had not gone into work that day, and came up with a plan. Here's what we decided, and I need to say it felt half-assed and dangerous to me.

We assumed that the cops had found out about the shooting in Harare, so there was a good chance they also knew about Sekuru. It was time to come clean with them. Piers was to arrange a meeting with Inspector Witherspoon, PC Jamison, Zuri, and me in his office. Getting the flatfoots there would be easy. He would tell them Zuri would be in Piers's office at two o'clock, eager to talk.

Zuri and I cooled our heels until one fifteen and then went to the hotel. We thought it better she ditch the gun in her hotel room safe before meeting with the Wigton law dogs. Besides, she wanted a change of clothes—she had been pretty much wearing the same thing plus my San Francisco sweats all the time at Kelly's. Kelly and Zuri thought it would be a bad idea for Kelly to go to her room and leave the hotel with an armful of clothes. Anyway, I gotta tell you, I didn't like going to her room, but she is one strong lady. I texted Piers to tell him we'd be in her room until just before two. At precisely 1:45 p.m., there was a knock at the door. I knew the time because I kept looking at the clock on the bedside table, anxious for two o'clock to come.

Zuri hesitated and then went slowly to look through the peephole. She turned to me and whispered, "It's Chantall!"

As she was turning back to the door, we heard Chantall's voice. It sounded like she was crying. "Zuri, it's me, Chantall. Open the door. We need to talk. I let you down, and I'm so sorry. Zuri, I loved Tawanda. Please. We're cousins. We've got history. I loved him."

So while I'm thinking, *How the hell does she know Zuri is here,* Zuri said, "She's crying, Drake." She slid the chain off, and before I could stop her, she began opening the door.

Suddenly someone smashed through the door with force, knocking Zuri back. She stumbled and hit the floor hard. The man had a gun in his right hand and pointed it at Zuri. I reacted without thinking, rushing forward and tackling him violently. As the man and I crashed into the wall, his gun went off. A slug hit the floor close to where Zuri lay. I felt the impact of the wall and then fell to the floor. The bastard lashed out at me, catching me in the face with the barrel of his gun. I felt something warm and wet running down my cheek. He was on his feet before I knew it, once again taking aim at Zuri.

Just as he was about to shoot, Inspector Witherspoon rushed into the room. His billy club slammed down on the man's arm. He dropped the gun, screaming in pain. I bet you could have heard the bone break all the way down the hall. The big man's eyes rolled up in his head. He went down, out cold.

PC Jamison and Piers had followed Witherspoon into the room. As Witherspoon went to Zuri's side, Jamison rolled the Zimbabwean onto his back and cuffed his hands. Piers knelt and put his handkerchief to my bloody face.

"Here, hold this," he said, moving my hand to my face. "I'll call Dr. Pritchard. You're going to need a few stitches."

Great, I thought, hoping the doc wasn't foot faulting on the tennis court.

"Are you okay, Ms. Manyika?" asked Inspector Witherspoon.

"Where's Chantall?" asked Zuri.

Zuri and I looked at each other. I saw both shock and relief in her eyes. She crawled across the floor to me and took the handkerchief and held it tightly to my face. "What the hell just happened?" she whispered in my ear.

Looking over to the cuffed man, now coming to his senses, I said, "I take it that bastard is Sekuru."

Before long more cops showed up with Chantall in tow. She had tried to run from the scene but ran right into the cops at the statue in the corridor. She and Sekuru were hauled away.

Doc Pritchard arrived and got to work on my face, saying I needed to get to his office to have the cut sewed up. I protested I wasn't going anywhere until I found out how Piers and the Wigton heat got to the room in time to save the freakin' day. Piers promised me he would fill me in if I let him drive me to the doc's office. And if truth be told, there wasn't much determination behind all my noise. I was in no mood to argue. A bit of cutting and sewing was in order.

So this was the lowdown as far as I could piece it together. Chantall was in cahoots with Sekuru and lured Zuri down to London to find out where she was staying. After Zuri returned to Silloth, Chantall and Sekuru rented a car and headed north. They found a quiet B&B outside Wigton, and it was Chantall who kept an eye on the Skinburness Hotel, waiting for Zuri to appear. In the meantime, Wigton's finest had discovered that Zuri had shot a man in Harare, but that she was not being pursued by Zimbabwean officials. The Harare cops couldn't—or wouldn't—explain why they'd dropped the case, and Witherspoon smelled a rat. No way did he want a Zimbabwean political revenge saga played out on his turf. The arrival of an African couple in Wigton had doubled his suspicions.

So unbeknownst to us all, Witherspoon too had been watching the Skinburness Hotel. When Zuri and I returned that morning, Witherspoon was already there in the parking lot. He saw us go in. Half an hour later he saw Sekuru and Chantall go in. He immediately called in the troops and then quietly followed the Zimbabweans to the second floor.

Piers was surprised when he looked out his window and saw three squad cars tear into the parking lot. He met them at the back entrance of the hotel and was right behind them when they charged up the stairs. The rest you know. I had obviously underestimated the Wigton police. Who would have thought?

And just to close the circle, I was right when I had thought Witherspoon would want to tidy things up. He quickly dismissed concerns about Johnny H. He went ahead and sent Zuri's ring to the lab. Results, no poison. As far as Witherspoon was concerned, case closed on Zuri, as it was case closed on mob hits. Only one thread left hanging: the volatile Lily Henderson. So I might as well tie that up for you too.

Lily Henderson might have turned out to be a racist bitch, but apparently she was no murderer. Witherspoon had the lab boys do a quick hunt for fingerprints, I think because her letter had been so violent. While her fingerprints were all over Tolentino's apartment, there was no evidence at all that she hid away in the front cloakroom, waiting for rescuers to force their way in when Tolentino didn't show the following day. Piers insisted that it was very unlikely she could have sneaked out when he had the handyman cut the chain and enter the apartment. But even if this unlikely scenario were possible, the Wigton coppers just couldn't believe Lily Henderson could have scared Tolentino to death. I mean, she could be pretty scary when mad, but not that scary.

So, as far as Inspector Ralph Witherspoon and the Carlisle coroner were concerned, it was case closed on Tolentino. Natural causes it would be until the sun stopped burning hydrogen and helium. Locked room mystery solved.

But given my conversation with Dr. Jaroslav Raich in Prague, I wasn't so sure. I had to admit to myself, and it was difficult, case still open on *The Woman in White Marble*. In the end, you gotta follow the story, no matter where it leads.

23

It took five stitches to close up my wound. Given that Dr. Pritchard kept saying it had been a long time since he stitched anyone, I was pretty sure there was a scar in my future. In the spirit of *mi casa es su casa*, Zuri moved in with me until she figured out her next step. I figured it would be right back to New Orleans. She was in the clear, and Sekuru was locked up in national and international legal complexities—and in an English cage—for some time to come. As for Chantall, well, she was in deep shit too, being an accomplice and all. Even after all that had happened, her fate lay heavy on Zuri's heart.

Five days had passed after the brouhaha in Zuri's hotel room when Libbie and Kara came a-knocking at my front door. I hadn't been down to the Skinburness and had only talked to Piers on the blower. I wanted to give my face some time to return to something approaching normal size. Besides, I was relishing being holed up with my utterly beautiful African princess. The girls, however, were calling time on my small oasis of healing, love, and sex.

To be honest, I didn't want to think about *The Woman in White Marble*. The law dogs had closed the case on Silvestre Tolentino, I was spending a lot of time in the arms of the best lover I had ever known, and anyway, the whole thing was just a legend. I hadn't seen anything in the hotel that night. Just light playing with me.

As far as the statue was concerned, well, yeah, it was unusually beautiful, sensual, and alluring, but it was made of cold, hard marble. I could see some men getting off on her, but I wasn't some men. I am Drake Ramsey, and I didn't need a woman in white when I had Zuri.

As I looked into Kara's and Libbie's accusing eyes, however, I shouted to myself, *Keep a grip, Drake!* They invited themselves up the stairs to my living quarters.

"You know it's not over," Libbie said very seriously. Damn if she wasn't just too old for her age.

"What do you mean, honey?" Zuri asked.

"Drake knows what I mean," Libbie said.

"Drake, you know she's right," Kara joined in.

"Oh God, you're not talking about the ghost thing," Zuri said, slightly annoyed.

"Girls, this is crazy," I said, almost pleading.

"You didn't honor our deal," Libbie said.

"You only stayed two nights and then headed up to London," Kara added.

Up to London. That always cracks me up. Apparently, wherever the natives are on this island, whenever they travel to London, they always say they are traveling "up" to the Big Smoke. How crazy is that? Go figure. But anyway, dear Kara. What could I do?

Kara was always so damn reasonable. And they were both good

kids. What harm could be done? I had no choice but to go back to room 217 for three more nights.

"Well, Drake. It is a nice room, nicer than the one I was staying in. You think Piers would mind if I joined you?" Zuri asked.

"No!" Libbie shouted. "You can't go. He has to be there alone. We've been over this. The ghost won't come to him if there's a woman with him. She goes after men when they're alone. Everyone knows that."

"She has a point," I said.

Zuri laughed and held her hands up in surrender.

And so that night I was back in room 217 in the Edwin Hodge Banks West Wing. A fire had been laid in the fireplace, and there was plenty of wood in the big basket. Jacklyn, bless her heart, had put a bottle of wine and some cheese and crackers on the table by the window. Propped up on the bottle of red was a card. It said, *Have a good sleep, and if you do see the Woman in White, give her my regards. Ha ha! Love, Jacklyn.*

I confess I was a little hurt, given the Woman in White's reputation as a ruthless killer. Where was the joke in that? But then I remembered that Jacklyn, while claiming to have seen the ghost, didn't hold to the stories of murder. Just a sad ghost woman wandering the west wing of the Skinburness Hotel.

It's obvious to you by now that I'm a big boy and that I know my way around. I've had my time with the bad guys and the ladies. Still, if forced to tell the truth and nothing but the truth, I was a little uneasy being back in room 217. Not far down the hall was *The Woman in White Marble*, standing there cold as ice. So I was back to thinking about a good montra.

The best I could come up with, since I really don't believe in spirits and ghosts and things like that, was, *Get a fucking grip, you idiot. Ghosts don't exist. No Woman in White is going to float out of The Woman* in White Marble, *come into your room, scare you to death, and then float back inside the statue.*

I thought about it for a moment and realized that was pretty damn long for a montra, so I shortened it. Saying my montra—*Get a fucking grip, you idiot. Ghosts don't exist*—over and over again, I set up my laptop on the desk and lit the fire. I was fully intending to write the denouement of Chad Steel's adventures across the galaxy and once and for all settle his relationship with the beautiful but dangerous Rashida.

Unfortunately, concentration was hard to come by, so I grabbed my Kindle and turned my attention to *The Haunting of Hill House*. I took the book as a kind of manly challenge, a way of facing my fears and all that. And, if I'm honest, I didn't want Parker to have the last laugh. So with my montra in mind I began reading.

"*Theodora touched the statue timidly, putting her fingers against the outstretched hand of one of the figures. 'Marble is always a shock,' she said. 'It never feels like you think it's going to. I suppose a life-size statue looks enough like a real person to make you expect to feel skin.'*"

I clicked off the Kindle and sat looking at the fire. Obviously, my mind kept wandering to the statue down the hall, under the glass roof. I couldn't help wondering if the marble felt like skin. I decided to bite the bullet and face some more of my fears.

Repeating my montra, I left the room and made my way down the hall. The light of the full moon was shining through the skylight, embracing *The Woman in White Marble*. She looked stunning and nonthreatening, perhaps even vulnerable. I stood in front of her and looked into her eyes. Her pure white face, slender and perfect. Her full lips ever so slightly parted, not in a smile but in a look of wonderment. Of course I had seen her before, but now her long hair falling over her right shoulder and down her back seemed soft, almost real. Her light, thin gown was like a robe you would see on a Greek or Roman goddess. Her bare shoulders, arms, and chest, her full breasts and nipples beneath the garment, were seductive. Her left leg, perfectly shaped, peeking out from her gown, aroused me. Her right arm by her side and her left across her stomach almost seemed to move. Her hands were perfect and fired the imagination.

As I stood there looking at her, I moved closer and put my left arm around her shoulder and my right hand on her breast. I leaned forward, and just as my lips touched the cool marble lips of *The Woman in White Marble*, I jolted as if released from a trance. I suddenly saw what I was doing and jumped back, mortified. I looked up and down the corridor to see if anyone had been watching. Thank God, I was alone. I quickly walked back toward my room, the whole time feeling the cool touch of her lips. They had felt soft.

When I got back in my room, I poked the fire with the heavy iron rod and put another log in the flames. I put the bottle of wine and a glass on the bedside table, then went to the bathroom and threw cold water over my face. I returned to the bed, poured a big glass of wine, undressed, and climbed into bed, leaving all the lights on. I normally sleep in the nude and saw no reason to change that night. There was no such thing as ghosts, and certainly not sexy ones! I turned on the TV for mindless distraction and drank.

At two, I woke. All the lights and the TV were still on, and I realized that I had fallen asleep watching the box. The fire had died. I turned off the lights and TV and curled up on my right side so I could see the door. Amazingly, I slept soundly.

The next morning, I awoke refreshed and went down to have breakfast with the Cullingworths. Piers and Jacklyn were damn good cooks, and they put on a spread to honor the occasion.

When I walked into the kitchen, I'm certain both Libbie

and Kara looked relieved, presumably because I wasn't dead! Of course, during the interrogation over scrambled eggs, sausage, toast, fresh orange juice, and a cup of joe, I failed to mention my brief encounter with the statue. Hell, I was beginning to think that I had imagined the whole thing or that it had been a dream. Yes, a dream. No doubt. What I did say was that I got a lot of writing done, read a little, watched TV, enjoyed the fire and wine, and then slept the sleep of the innocent. Close enough, don't you think?

The rest of the day was uneventful. Suffice it to say that Zuri and I recovered her car and drove down to Windermere to have a look around. The weather was glorious. Zuri bought me a bottle of single malt in a wine store. A little warmth for the cold night ahead, as she put it. We walked down to the lake and took a boat ride. That evening we had dinner in the hotel restaurant, as paying customers I should add, and then went up to my room. We gave the bed a good workout, and Zuri left about nine o'clock, the scent of her lingering on the sheets.

After she left, I stoked up the fire and poured myself a whiskey. I didn't feel like writing, leaving Chad Steel and Rashida, who had shuttled up to the *Liberté C57-D* from Betelgeuse in the Omicron^2 Centauri System for a secure place to plan their next moves, but instead did the dirty in zero gravity. I pulled the soft chair and the table from the window over to the fireplace, then settled down with the whisky and *The Haunting of Hill House*.

I read for a good hour and a half. Apparently, the glorious weather I had mentioned passed out of sight, for I could hear the wind howling and the rain beating against the curtained window. Somehow it was pleasant, listening to the storm outside as I put another log on the fire. I poured myself another whisky, a small one, and just watched the fire. I thought I heard someone walking in the hallway, but put it down to the wind. I was the only one in the Edwin Hodge Banks West Wing, after all.

As the whisky took hold, I was tempted to pay *The Woman in White Marble* another visit, but decided against it. I took a shower and then climbed into bed. Feeling safe, I curled up on my left side, facing the window. I got up again and opened the curtains about halfway so I could see and hear the rain hitting the window. I was asleep within minutes.

I suddenly opened my eyes. I was still on my left side, and the rain was still banging against the window; the wind sounded fierce. I did not know what had woken me. I supposed the sound of the storm, but then I noticed in the black window a light image. For a second I thought I was looking at something, perhaps someone, outside the window looking in at me, which didn't make a lot of sense since I was on the second floor of the hotel. Then suddenly I realized with a shock that I was looking at a reflection. Of course I was. I didn't move and tried to calm my breathing. As my eyes cleared of sleep, I saw that the room was somehow eerily illumined. I heard a slight rustle of clothing and watched the reflection in the window lean toward me, reaching out a hand. I slowly rolled over on my back, and there she was—the Woman in White!

She tilted her head, looked at me, and drew her hand back. Then, unbelievably, she smiled. "I've been looking for you," she said softly, lovingly.

She glowed a soft, extremely pleasant white. It was not that she was surrounded by light; she *was* light. I could clearly see her naked body beneath her transparent garment. Her hair moved gently as she tilted her head even further to the left, looking at me deeply. She took my breath away. She was by far more beautiful, alluring, and sensual than the statue. She was light. She was warmth. She was everything I could ever imagine wanting in a woman.

I sat up in bed, realizing that I was becoming aroused. I wasn't frightened at all, but was drawn to her. My arousal didn't embarrass me. It was totally fitting. The Woman in White must have sensed my feelings and enthusiasm because she moved forward and sat on the bed. She was light *and* substance. Her scent embraced me. Her warmth touched me. I removed the blanket and sheet and slid closer to her. She said, "I want you," and leaned forward to kiss me. She placed her hand on my stomach. Just as her warm, moist lips touched mine, my cell phone rang.

The sound was jarring. The Woman in White pulled back suddenly, angrily, and stood up. The cell continued to ring. It sounded abnormally loud. She turned and, right before my eyes, walked through the door. I got up, ran to the door, opened it, and looked down the hall. She was nowhere in sight. I ran through the hallway until I came to the statue and stopped cold. As I watched, standing there as naked as the day I was born, the Woman in White melded back into the marble and was gone. The Woman in White and *The Woman in White Marble* were one.

I just stood there, but I could feel that I was slowly regaining my sense of perspective. I started feeling exposed in my nakedness. The hall was cold. The rain beating down on the skylight seemed violent. The wind began to frighten me. And my cell stopped ringing, no doubt going to voice mail.

I returned to my room, closed and locked the door, though a fat lot of good that would do, and climbed back in bed. The cell phone bleeped, indicating I had a voice message. I propped myself against the headboard, turned on the lights by the bed, and listened to the message.

It was Zuri. She apologized for calling so late. I looked quickly at the bedside clock, and the red numbers indicated it was 2:36 a.m. She said she had started feeling uncomfortable and felt compelled to call, supposed I had turned the sound off my cell or was sleeping through the ring tone, and then closed by saying, *Drake, listen, I think I love you, so take care. Zuri.*

I didn't know what to do. In the end, I stayed sitting up in bed with the lights on until the sun started to come up. At the first sight of light, I slid down under the covers and went to sleep.

24

I heard a knocking on the door and Libbie calling my name. I got up, grabbed the hotel robe from the closet, and opened the door. There was Piers with that smile of his, the one that both warmed and teased you. "We were worried about you," he said.

Libbie and Kara stood there staring at me. Their looks of concern visibly mutated into looks of confident acknowledgment before my eyes.

"You saw her last night. I know you did," Kara said.

"Don't be silly. I ... I had a restless night and overslept," I said.

"Yeah, right!" Libbie said. "Well, Mum's got some coffee and croissants if you want. You can tell us all about it."

"Let me shower and dress at least. Okay?"

"Yeah, right!" Libbie said.

Piers ushered the girls away. In short order I was sitting at the kitchen table with Jacklyn, Kara, Libbie, and Zuri, who had just walked in the front door of the Skinburness as Piers and the girls were coming down the main stairs. Zuri was clearly ill at ease and not wanting to be sitting around the family Cullingworth table. Basil nuzzled up to her side, but it didn't help. She ignored him.

To say the least, I was subdued. As I drank my coffee, the previous night began to feel like a dream. I mean, was it a dream? It had the quality of dreams: surreal, trancelike, and yet vivid, surprising, sexual, with a sudden awakening and a lingering impression left on the mind and heart that the morning sun slowly dissolved.

Anyway, that's the story I told at the table, but mind you, without the intimate details. Just that in my dream I saw an apparition one might think was a woman who might have resembled the statue under the skylight. Libbie's only comment was, "Well, we'll see what happens tonight." Kara looked through me with those wonderfully intelligent and trusting eyes. Jacklyn . . . well, she just laughed at me. She had, after all, seen the Woman in White herself.

Zuri and I left the hotel quietly, but we both knew what was on the other person's mind, and it wasn't a white female ghost. It was a voice mail message.

As we stepped out of the hotel, the air felt crisp and clear. The ground was washed clean and bright. As I breathed in the air and felt the sun on my face, the intensity of experience of the night faded. We decided to walk.

"I assume you got my message," Zuri said almost hesitantly, which was not like her. Zuri was an intelligent and confident person with a body to die for. I just kept walking, not knowing what to say. I mean, how could a woman like Zuri go for a man like me? The idea was almost as absurd as ghosts.

"Well, say something," she said. "That message was tough for me. I don't know where I stand with you. As far as I know, you're just another white boy wanting some black ass."

Now that hurt. I'm no prince, but …

She saw the pain in my profile and said, "I'm sorry. That wasn't fair."

"No, it wasn't. And yes, I did get your call. It woke me from that dream I was having," I said, still looking at the ground as we walked.

"Well, why didn't you answer?" she said, stopping and turning me to face her. "I don't know whether to be humiliated or expectant. I'm not even sure that I meant what I said."

There was absolutely no breeze, and I could hear Zuri breathing. She stood there looking straight at me with her hands tucked in her coat pockets. I didn't know what to say. What with a ghost trying to seduce me and all, I hadn't even begun to sort out my thoughts and feelings about the message. Part of me was thrilled. My God, this magnificent woman had said she loved me. Or rather, that she thought she loved me, which I guess is a big difference. Talk about climbing out onto a freakin' limb.

I reached into her coat pockets and held her hands. Their warmth was reassuring. I said, "This is happening kind of fast, but I want it to. I think I love you too, or if I don't, I'm pretty damn close. It's all a bit scary. I mean, are we saying we love each other because we love each other, or to try to make it real? I guess I don't want to hear those words from you and then have them withdrawn. Does that make sense to you?"

She looked slightly skeptical but was smiling.

"Zuri, do you want to create this thing between us?" I asked, dead serious.

She never hesitated, which frankly was a good sign. "Yes, I do, though at this point I don't know where it's leading. Do you?"

"No. Not a clue."

"Well then, let's just go with it."

"Let's." And then she kissed me.

The day was great. We drove into Carlisle and had lunch at Watt's & Sons and then just wandered around. When we got back to Silloth, Zuri suggested we go back to the hotel, but I insisted we go to my place. After the previous night's encounter, dream or real, I felt uncomfortable at the thought of being in room 217 with Zuri. We made dinner and then love. I lingered as long as I could and then got into my bird-shit-covered car and drove to the Skinburness.

As soon as I walked into room 217, I felt her presence. No, she wasn't there, but the entire atmosphere in the room was heavy with the previous night's experience.

I didn't lock the door. Why bother? I lit a fire, turned on my laptop, but didn't even pretend to write. I poured myself a whisky and sat by the fire with my Kindle in my lap. I didn't have the heart to turn to *The Haunting of Hill House*. Shirley Jackson had written a really scary book! I decided to let Parker laugh all he wanted to.

At midnight I undressed and climbed into bed. I propped the pillows up against the headboard and made myself comfortable. I turned out all the lights and stared at the door. I waited.

I suddenly opened my eyes and looked up. I had fallen asleep. Of course, she was there. Her light had woken me. She was standing at the foot of the bed, smiling at me.

"I've missed you," she said lovingly. I believed her. "I want you tonight. I will love you tonight."

She moved from the end of the bed and lay down beside me. I removed the blanket and she looked at me seductively. She leaned closer, and her breasts brushed against my chest. She kissed me and gently held my penis in her right hand. We kissed slowly and sensually. I pulled her to me as I slid down from the headboard. She lay by my side, her left leg over mine pulling us closer together. I felt her body pushing against mine and her lips kissing my chest and her breathing in and out until it matched mine. In and out. In and out. I was in ecstasy.

She continued to breathe lusciously but now with her lips on mine. Her hand holding my penis gripped me tighter and tighter until I was in considerable pain. Suddenly I awoke as if from a spell. I opened my eyes and looked into hers.

"Oh, come now. You're not going to complain about a little pain. Pain is good. Pain is exciting. Don't you like that?" she said, looking into my eyes and squeezing me even tighter. "You will love this," she continued, now not as a seductress, but as an aggressor.

I did not see beauty in her eyes anymore, but lust and hatred. While her mouth was very close to mine, our lips were no longer touching. I realized she was no longer breathing in and out but drawing breath from my lungs. I made as if to grab her shoulders and push her off, but I couldn't move. I became frightened and then very quickly terrified. The more terrified I became, the more lustful became her smile.

"Just relax. If you don't fight me, you will enjoy it," she said in a rough, almost masculine voice. My heart was pounding, and my insides were exploding, but I still couldn't move. She kept looking into my eyes and pulling the life out of me. It felt as though my heart was going to burst.

As if from a distance, I heard the door open with force and slam against the wall. At first I didn't know what was happening. Zuri rushed into the room. She grabbed the Woman in White's long hair, pulled her off me, and threw her to the floor. I lifted myself up on my elbows and saw the Woman in White get up and step back from Zuri, who had positioned herself between me and the apparition. The Woman in White rushed toward us, and Zuri slapped her hard across the face. She stopped dead in her tracks and then took a step back. The room was still and silent for what seemed like an eternity.

Then suddenly the Woman in White screamed and ran forward again, and again Zuri hit her across the face.

The Woman in White stopped and, looking at Zuri, said, "You protect this man?"

"Yes," Zuri said defiantly.

"But he is a man!" said the Woman in White with strength.

"Yes," Zuri said with sadness in her voice. "Yes, he is."

"He is a man," the Woman in White said again but this time quietly, the strength leaving her voice.

"Yes; a man I love," Zuri said with tenderness.

The Woman in White was silent. Then suddenly her face was transformed into complete and utter beauty, clearly by an act of remembrance. It was a beauty fundamentally different from that of the seductress. Just as suddenly, she began to weep. Her head fell to her chest, her entire body shook, and it looked as though she was about to fall to the floor.

Zuri stepped forward quickly and held the Woman in White in her arms. She slowly kissed her forehead and her eyelids, and drank in her tears. She ever so gently kissed the Woman in White's lips until the crying stopped.

The Woman in White stepped back and said to Zuri, "You must kill the marble. Please. I cannot."

Realizing my strength had returned, I jumped off the bed, grabbed the iron fireside poker, and ran out of the room and down the hall to the glass corridor, naked and angry. When I reached the sculpture, I raised the poker. But just as I was going to strike, I heard Zuri shouting, "Stop! It can't be you! *Stop!*"

I turned my head and saw Zuri and the Woman in White rushing toward me. As soon as I heard the shouting, I realized what I was about to do and lowered the poker. Zuri came up to me, snatched the poker from my hands, and began striking the head of the sculpture with all her strength. The Woman in White stood in the corridor, watching. Zuri continued hitting the head until it broke in two and fell to the floor, shattering in a thousand pieces. She looked at the pieces at her feet and then began striking the body of the statue, breaking off the arms, the left leg, striking with all her strength until a crack appeared around the figure's waist. With one last, mighty blow, Zuri knocked the statue to the floor, where it broke into fragments and dust.

She turned to the Woman in White with sweat and dust on her face, with a look of both hatred and satisfaction. The Woman in White smiled radiantly and said, "My name is Sobêska."

As we watched, Sobêska began to melt into particles of light, a billion photons swirling and flowing together upward through the skylight and into the black night, into nothingness.

I turned to Zuri, and the hatred in her face was fading. I had, for a moment, feared that hatred was directed at me, and I said, "I'm sorry for what I was about to do. But Zuri, I get it."

She smiled at me and said, "No need. I killed the fucking bastard." She then took my hand and we walked back to room 217.

Zuri took me to the bathroom and undressed. We stood naked before each other and then walked into the shower and let the hot water run down our bodies. After a long time, we dried ourselves, climbed into bed, and held each other. We fell asleep without another word being spoken.

25

"You're not going to believe what happened, but at least there won't be any more mysterious deaths in the Skinburness Hotel," I said to Piers, Jacklyn, Libbie, Kara, Parker, and Kelly.

"Sorry about the statue," Zuri said to Piers.

We were all sitting around a large, round table in the hotel restaurant. Zuri and I had decided it was best to get everyone together for lunch so the story would only have to be told once. And tell it we did.

Piers and Parker remained skeptical to the last, though they couldn't imagine why we would have fabricated such a story. Skeptical or not, however, late that afternoon they hauled the broken pieces of *The Woman in White Marble* behind the hotel and smashed them to bits with a sledgehammer. They then shoveled the pieces into a large, black, plastic garbage can and took it to a dump far away from the Skinburness Hotel. It reminded me of that saying "I don't believe in ghosts, but they scare the shit out of me."

Jacklyn and Kelly nodded throughout the telling as if the story simply verified what they already knew. They obviously thought no comment was necessary, for they made none.

Kara and Libbie? Well, they were both shocked and brave. And, of course, vindicated. I should add, this time I didn't spare their youthful innocence and told the *entire* story. They had started this whole thing, so it was only right they heard how it ended. They lived.

As for me, well, on the *Fremont Argus News* we tell it straight and true. I didn't change my modus operandi simply because this story took me down pathways unexpected.

You would have thought the damn sun would shine to celebrate our victory over darkness and all that, but no. The rain came down in sheets. The wind blew. The grayness mocked our triumph. What can I say? This is Silloth on the Solway Firth. Nonetheless, victory it was.

A couple of days after my almost fatal encounter with the Woman in White, Kelly dropped a note through my door. It said this:

Dear Zuri and Drake,

I thought you would like to know that the Czech name Sobêska means She is Glorious.

Love,
Kelly

EPILOGUE

It felt great sharing my house with Zuri, but we both knew it couldn't last. Given that Silvestre Tolentino's death was signed off as due to natural causes, that Johnny H, Lily Henderson, and Zuri were cleared, that Sekuru was going to spend a long, long time in an English jail, and that Sobêska had been liberated from her prison of violence, there was nothing to stop Zuri from returning to Loyola University. So I figured if I could travel all the way to Prague to chase down a white ghost, I could also tell my African princess how I felt. It would cost a bundle, but I figured Grandma would consider it money well spent. I mean, we were talking about Zuri here.

First, I washed the bird shit off the red death trap I affectionately called my car. Then, taking Parker's advice, I booked us a reservation for dinner and a room for the night at the Sharrow Bay on Lake Ullswater. I asked for a private table, and private is what I got. When Zuri and I arrived in the dining room, wearing our Sunday best,

169

we were ushered into a small room with a table for two. One whole wall was a window looking out on Lake Ullswater. There was even a door to shut out the noise of the other diners. Talk about class.

I waited until dessert and then told all, dumping my guts in a less than self-assured and sophisticated manner. What can I say? The stakes were high. But by all the gods we human beings have ever created, it worked. We showed no mercy on the bedsheets that night, let me tell you. And we came up with a plan.

Zuri headed back to New Orleans while I stayed on in Wettown-on-the-Solway to finish writing *The Woman in Blue Skies*. Once it's finished and digitally saved, I will head off to New Orleans and look for a job on a local rag or try my hand at being a full-time novelist. God knows there is a story in *The Woman in White Marble*, though I'd have to turn the whole damn thing into fiction. I mean, who would believe me?

And so I called my editor in Fremont and ruined his day. It was good-bye to the *Fremont Argus News* and hello to the vagaries of life on the edge.

It was hard saying good-bye to Zuri. I rode the train with her down to London, where we got a purple room near Euston Station. The next day I taxied with her to Heathrow and said, "See you later," in as manly a fashion as I could muster.

I'm now back in my front room, standing in the bay window. My laptop is sitting on the arm of the chair, and a cup of joe is sending vapors toward the ceiling. Outside, Dr. Pritchard is foot faulting like there is no tomorrow. Once again there is bird shit on my red car, and the fine gray mist is gathering weight. It will be raining soon. Later it's down to the Skinburness Hotel for a couple of pints and bangers and mash, as the natives call it. It'll be Kelly, Parker, and me tonight. On me—or, more accurately, on Grandma.

But for now, it's time to write. I've gotta get out of this

who-gives-a-fuck-sunset town and back into the arms of Dr. Zuri Manyika. And though I'm more than a little apprehensive about the future, we've got more plans to make.

In the midst of all this, I have written the great Proustian science fiction novel. Poor Piers is going to have a fit when he discovers I've populated the galaxy with a bunch of Frenchies. But what the hell; it's my novel, and he'll get over it. And as it turns out, Chad Steel loves madeleine sponge cake. He can't get enough of that shit.

In Proust's last volume, *Finding Time Again*, Charles Swann found it nice to see so much green from his bedroom window. I figure Chad Steel deserves the same. It's time to take him home. So ...

Chad Steel will discover that Agnians are more real than imaginary. He will do battle with their representative and, of course, be victorious. The battle will be fierce, but Chad Steel will never lose his resolve or his faith in his own abilities. He will be cut and bruised, but in the end the Agnian will be vanquished, disassembled into a billion particles, and driven back into subspace. Needless to say, Chad Steel's triumph over the heartless assassin and legendary being from another galaxy will both solve the murder of S. T. and prevent a full-scale invasion of our galaxy by the Agnians.

After the battle that rages throughout S. T.'s mansion, Chad Steel will exit the front door to find the Betelgeuse authorities and not a small number of its population applauding his victory. But in front of them all will be a blue beauty, pistol and blade secure, standing with a smirk on her face. She will say, "So, man enough to kill an Agnian, I see. But are you man enough to take me?"

Chad Steel will laugh loudly, walk forward, and roughly pull Rashida to his battle-worn body. He will look into her pearl-green eyes and say, "Need you really ask, my blue wonder?"

They will kiss hard and long, and then, hand in hand, they will step into the shuttle waiting to deliver them to the *Liberté C57-D.* Chad Steel's second in command will ask, "Where to, Captain?"

"Let's set sail for the Orion Nebula for a little fun," he'll say, "and then home to Sol. Rashida and I have plans to make."

Lightning Source UK Ltd.
Milton Keynes UK
UKOW02f0844280914

239284UK00001B/39/P

9 781491 742815